EQUOID

EQUOID

A Laundry Files Novella

Charles Stross

SUBTERRANEAN PRESS 2014

First Edition

ISBN
978-1-59606-664-9

Subterranean Press
PO Box 190106
Burton, MI 48519

subterraneanpress.com

BOB! ARE YOU busy right now? I'd like a moment of your time."

Those thirteen words never bode well—although coming from my new manager, Iris, they're less doom-laden than if they were falling from the lips of some others I could name. In the two months I've been working for her Iris has turned out to be the sanest and most sensible manager I've had in the past five years. Which is saying quite a lot, really, and I'm eager to keep her happy while I've got her.

"Be with you in ten minutes," I call through the open door of my office; "got a query from HR to answer first." Human Resources have teeth, here in the secretive branch of the British government known to its inmates as the Laundry; so when HR ask you to do their homework—ahem, provide one's opinion of an applicant's suitability for a job opening—you give them priority over your regular work load. Even when it's pretty obvious that they're taking the piss.

I am certain that Mr. Lee would make an extremely able addition to the Office Equipment Procurement Team, I type, *if he was not already*—according to your own goddamn database, if you'd bothered to check it—*a lieutenant in the Chinese Peoples Liberation Army Jiangshi Brigade.* Who presumably filled out the shouldn't-have-been-published-on-the-internet job application on a drunken dare, or to test our vetting procedures, or something. *Consequently I suspect that he would fail our mandatory security background check at the first hurdle.* (As long as the vetting officer isn't *also* a PLA mole.)

I hit "send" and wander out into the neon tube overcast where Iris is tapping her toes. "Your place or mine?"

"Mine," says Iris, beckoning me into her cramped corner office. "Have a chair, Bob. Something's come up, and I think it's right up your street." She plants herself behind her desk, leans back in her chair, and preps her pitch. "It'll get you out of the office for a bit, and if HR are using you to stomp all over the dreams of upwardly-mobile Chinese intelligence operatives it means you're—"

"Underutilized. Yeah, whatever." I wave it off. But it's true: since I sorted out the funny stuff in the basement at St. Hilda's I've been *bored.* The day-to-day occupation of the average secret agent mostly consists of hurry up and wait. In my case, that means filling in on annoying bits of administrative scutwork and handling upgrades to the departmental network—when I'm not being called upon to slay multi-tentacled horrors from beyond spacetime. (Which doesn't happen very often, actually, for which I am profoundly grateful.) "You said it's out of the office?"

"Yes." She smiles; she knows she's planted the hook. "A bit of fresh country air, Bob—you're too pallid. But tell me—" she leans forward—"what do you know about horses?"

The equine excursion takes me by surprise. "Uh?" I shake my head. "Four legs, hooves, and a bad attitude?" Iris shakes her head, so I try again: "Go with a carriage like, er, love and marriage?"

"No, Bob, I was wondering—did you ever learn to ride?"

"What, you mean—wait, we're not talking about bicycles here, right?" From her reaction I don't think that's the answer she was looking for. "I'm a city boy. As the photographer said, you should never work with animals or small children if you can avoid it. What's come up, a dressage emergency?"

"Not exactly." Her smile fades. "It's a shame, it would have made this easier."

"Made *what* easier?"

"I could have sworn HR said you could ride." She stares at me pensively. "Never mind. Too late to worry about has-beens now. Hmm. Anyway, it probably doesn't matter—you're married, so I don't suppose you're a virgin, either. Are you?"

"Get away!" *Virgins?* That particular myth is associated with unicorns, which don't exist, any more than vampires, dragons, or mummies—although I suppose if you wrapped a zombie in bandages you'd get a—*stop that.* In my head, confused stories about Lady Godiva battle with media images of tweed-suited shotgun-wielding farmers. "Do you need someone who can ride? Because I don't think I can learn in—"

"No, Bob, I need *you*. Or rather, the Department for Environment, Food and Rural Affairs needs a liaison officer who just happens to have your background and proven track record in—" she waves her left hand—"putting down infestations."

"Do they?" I do a double-take at *putting down infestations.* "Are they *sure* that's what they need?"

"Yes, they are. Or rather, they know that when they spot certain signs, they call us." She pulls open a desk drawer and removes a slim folder, its cover bearing the Crowned Portcullis emblem beneath an elder sign. "Take this back to your office and read it," she tells me. "Return it to the stacks when you're done. Then you can spend the rest of the afternoon thinking of ways to politely tell HR to piss up a rope, because tomorrow morning you're getting on a train to Hove in order to lend a DEFRA inspector a helping hand."

"You're serious?" I boggle at her. "You're sending me to do what? Inspect a farm?"

"I don't want to prejudice your investigation. There's a livery stable. Just hook up with the man from *The Archers*, take a look around, and phone home if anything catches your attention."

She slides the file across my desk and I open the flyleaf. It starts with TOP SECRET and a date round about the Battle of the Somme, crossed out and replaced with successively lower classifications until fifteen years ago it was marked down to MILDLY EMBARRASSING NO TABLOIDS. Then I flip the page and spot the title. "Hang on—"

"Shoo," she says, a wicked glint in her eyes. "Have fun!"

I shoo, smarting. I know a set-up when I see one—and I've been conned.

To UNDERSTAND WHY I knew I'd been tricked, you need to know who I am and what I do. Assuming you've read this far without your eyeballs boiling in your skull, it's probably safe to tell you that my name's Bob Howard—at least, for operational purposes; true names have power, and we don't like to give extradimensional identity thieves the keys to our souls—and I work for a secret government agency known to its inmates as the Laundry. It morphed into its present form during the Second World War, ran the occult side of the conflict with the Thousand Year Reich, and survives to this day as an annoying blob somewhere off to the left on the org chart of the British intelligence services, funded out of the House of Lords black budget.

Magic is a branch of applied mathematics, and I started out studying computer science (which is no more about computers than astronomy is about building really big telescopes). These days I specialize in applied computational demonology and general dogsbody work around my department. The secret service has never really worked out how to deal with people like me, who aren't admin personnel but didn't come up through the Oxbridge civil service fast-track route. In fact, I got into this line of work entirely by accident: if your dissertation topic leads you in the wrong direction you'd better hope that the Laundry finds you and makes you a job offer you can't refuse before the things you've unintentionally summoned up get bored talking to you and terminate your *viva voce* with prejudice.

After a couple of years of death by bureaucratic snu-snu (too many committee meetings, too many tedious IT admin jobs) I volunteered for active duty, without any clear understanding that it would mean *more* years of death by boredom (too many committee meetings, too many tedious IT jobs) along with a side-order of mortal terror courtesy of tentacle monsters from beyond spacetime.

As I am now older and wiser, not to mention married and still in possession of my sanity, I prefer my work life to be boringly predictable these days. Which it is, as a rule, but then along come the nuisance jobs—the Laundry equivalent of the way the US Secret Service always has to drop round for coffee, a cake, and a brisk interrogation with idiots who boast about shooting the president on Yahoo! Chat.

In my experience, your typical scenario is that some trespassing teenagers get stoned on 'shrooms, hallucinate flying saucers piloted by alien colorectal surgeons looking to field-test their new alien endoscope technology, and shit themselves copiously all over Farmer Giles' back paddock. A report is generated by the police, and as happens with reports of unknown origin, it accretes additional bureaucratic investigatory mojo until by various pathways it lands on the desk of one of our overworked analysts. They then bump it up the management chain and/or play cubicle ping-pong with it, because they're too busy working to keep tabs on the Bloody Skull Cult or cases of bovine demonic possession in Norfolk or something equally important. Finally, in an attempt to make the blessed thing *go away*, a manager finds a spare human resource and details the poor bastard to wade through the reports, interview the culprits, and then tread in cow shit while probing the farm cesspool for the spoor of alien pre-endoscopy laxatives. Nineteen times out of twenty it's an annoying paper chase followed by a day spent typing up a report that nobody will read. One time in twenty the affair is enlivened by you falling head-first into the cesspit. And the worst part of it is knowing that while you're off on a wild goose chase so you can close the books on the report, your everyday workload is quietly piling up in your in-tray and overflowing onto your desk...

Which is why, as I get back to my office, close the door, light up the DO NOT DISTURB sign, and open the folder Iris gave me, I start to swear quietly.

What the hell do the love letters of that old fraud H. P. Lovecraft have to do with the Department for Environment, Food and Rural Affairs?

Dear Robert,

I received your letter with, I must confess, some trepidation, not to mention mixed feelings of hope & despair tempered by the forlorn hope that the uncanny and unpleasant history of my own investigations & their regrettable outcome will serve to dampen the ardor with which you pursue your studies. I know full well to my great & abiding dismay the compulsive fascination that the eldritch & uncanny may exert upon the imagination of an introspective & sensitive scholar. I cannot help but be aware that you are already cognizant of the horrible risks to which your sanity will be exposed. What you may not be aware of is the *physical* damage that may fall upon you pursuant to these studies. It took my grandfather's life; it drove my father to seek redress by means of such vile & unmentionable acts that I cannot bring myself to record their nature for posterity—but suffice to say that his life was shortened thereby—and it has been grievously injurious to my own health & fitness for marriage. There, I say it baldly; but for the blessed Sonia I might have been a mortal wreck for my entire life. It was only by her grace & infinite patience that I regained some modicum of that which is the birthright of all the sons of Adam, and though we are parted she bears my guilty secret discreetly.

I confess that I was not always thus. My childhood was far from unhappy. I grew up an accident-prone but happy youth, living with my mother & my aunts in reduced but nevertheless genteel circumstances in Providence town. At first I studied the classics: Greek & Roman & Egyptian were my mother tongues, & all the rhapsodies of the poetic calling were mine! My grandfather's library was the orchid whose nectar I sipped, sweeter by far than any wine. He had amassed a considerable archive over the course of many years of travel inflicted on him by the base necessity of trade—I must interject at this juncture that I cannot stress too highly the need to shun such distractions as commerce if one is to reach one's full potential as a scholar by traversal of the path you propose to embark upon—and the fruits of his sorrows fermented into a heady vintage in time for my youthful excursions into his cellar to broach the casks of wisdom. However, I came to recognize a bitter truth as I assayed the dregs of his collection: my kindred souls are as the dust of the church-yard. As with Poe so am I one with the dead, for we persons of rarefied spirit & talent tread but seldom upon the boards of earth & are summoned all too soon to the exit eternal.

Now, as to the qualities of the MS submitted with your latest missive for my opinion, I must thank you most kindly for granting me the opportunity to review the work at this early stage—

I go home nursing a headache and a not inconsiderable sense of resentment at, variously: Iris for tricking me into this job; DEFRA for asking for back-up in the first place; and Howard Phillips Lovecraft of Providence, Rhode Island, for cultivating a florid and overblown prose style that covered the entire spectrum from purple to ultraviolet and took sixteen volumes of interminable epistles to get to the point—whatever point it was that constituted the meat of the EQUESTRIAN RED SIRLOIN dossier, which point I had not yet ascertained despite asymptotically approaching it in the course of reading what felt like reams & volumes of the aforementioned purple prose— *which is infectious.*

To cap it all, my fragrant wife Mo is away on some sort of assignment she can't talk about. All I know is that something's come up in Blackpool that requires her particular cross-section of very expensive talents, so I'm on my own tonight. (Combat epistemologists and violin soloists both are underpaid, but take many years and no little innate talent to train. Consequently, the demands on her time are many.) So I kick back with a bottle of passable cabernet sauvignon and a DVD—in this case, plucked at random from the watch-this-later shelf. It turns out to be a Channel Four production of *Equus*, by Peter Shaffer.

Which I am hitherto unfamiliar with (don't laugh: my background veers towards the distaff side of the Two Cultures) and which *really* doesn't mix well with a bottle of red wine and H. P. Lovecraft's ghastly prose. So I spend half the night tossing and turning to visions of melting spindly-legged Dali horses with gouged eye sockets—I've got to stop the eyeballs rolling away, for some reason—with the skin-crawling sense that something unspeakable is watching me from the back of the stables. This is bad enough that I then spend the second half of the night sitting at the kitchen table in my pajamas, brute-forcing my way through my half of my annual ideological self-criticism session—that is, the self-assessed goals and objectives portion of my performance appraisal—because the crawling horrors of human resources are far less scary than the gory movie playing out behind my eyeballs.

(This is why many of my co-workers eventually start taking work home—at least, the non-classified bits. Bureaucracy is a bulwark of comforting routine in the face of the things you really don't want to think about too hard by dead of night. Not to mention being a safer tranquilizer than drink or drugs.)

In my experience it's best to go on-site and nail these bullshit jobs immediately, rather than wasting too much time on over-planning. This one is, when all is said and done, what our trans-Atlantic cousins call "a snipe hunt." I'm hoping to nail it shut—probably a little girl with a strap-on plastic horn for her pony—and be home in time for tea. So the next morning I leave home and head straight for London Bridge station rather than going in to the office. I fight my way upstream through the onrushing stream of suits and catch the commuter train that carried them into London on its return journey, rattling and mostly empty on its run out to the dormitory towns of East Sussex.

It's just me and the early birds taking the cheapskate stopping service to Crapwick to avoid the hordes of holiday-makers (and pickpockets) at Thiefrow. And that's the way I like it.

I have a name and destination in the Request for Support memo Iris gave me: we're to investigate one G. Edgebaston, of Edgebaston Farm Livery Stables, near Hove. But first I'm supposed to meet a Mr. Scullery at a local DEFRA office in East Grinstead. Which is on the London to Brighton line, but it'll take me a good hour of start-stop commuter rail and then a taxi ride of indeterminate length to get there. So I take a deep breath and dive back into the regrettably deathless prose of the Prophet of Providence.

LISTEN, I KNOW what you're thinking.

You're probably thinking WHAT THE HELL, H. P. LOVECRAFT? And wondering why I'm reading his private letters (most certainly not found in any of the collections so lovingly curated by Lovecraft scholars over the years, from August Derleth to S. T. Joshi), in a file so mind-numbingly trivial that its leakage on the front page of a major tabloid newspaper would be greeted with snores.

This is the Laundry, after all, and we write memos and file expense reports every day that deal with gibbering horrors, things that go bump in the night, the lunatical followers of N'yar lath-Hotep, the worshippers of the Sleeper in the Pyramid, alien undersea and lithospheric colonies of BLUE HADES and DEEP SIX, and Old Bat Wings himself.

You probably think HPL was one of ours, or that maybe one of our predecessor agencies bumped him off, or that these letters contain Great & Terrible Mysteries, Secrets, & Eldritch

Wisdom of the Ancients and must be handled with asbestos tongs while reading them through welders' goggles. Right?

Well, you would be wrong. Although it's not your fault. You'd be wrong for the same reason as the folks who think modern fly-by-wire airliners can fly themselves from takeoff to landing (who needs pilots?), that Saddam really *did* have weapons of mass destruction (we just didn't search hard enough), and that the Filler of Stockings who brings presents down the chimney every Newtonmas-eve is a benign and cheery fellow. You've been listening to the self-aggrandizing exaggerations of self-promotion artists: respectively, the PR might of the airliner manufacturers, dodgy politicians, and the greeting card industry.

And so it is with old HPL: the very model of an 18th century hipster, born decades too late to be one of the original louche laudanum-addicted romantic poets, and utterly unafraid to bore us by droning on and on about the essential crapness of culture since Edgar Allan Poe, the degeneracy of the modern age, &c. &c. &c.

His reputation has been vastly inflated—out of all proportion—by his followers, who think he is the one true wellspring of wisdom concerning the Elder Gods, the Stars Coming Right, and various hideous horrors with implausible names like Shub-Niggurath, the goat of a thousand young, who spawns mindlessly on the darkest depths of the forest…

…Whereas, in actual fact, his writings are the occult equivalent of *The Anarchist Cookbook*.

It's absolutely true that Lovecraft *knew* stuff. Somewhere in grandpa's library he got his hands on the confused rambling inner doctrines of a dozen cults and secret societies. Most of these secrets were arrant nonsense on stilts—admixed with just enough knowledge to be deadly dangerous. Occultists of old, like the alchemists who poisoned themselves with mercury in their enthusiasm to transform lead into gold (meanwhile missing the opportunity to invent the modern discipline of chemistry as we understand it), didn't know much. What they *did* know was mostly just enough to guarantee a slow, lingering death from Krantzberg Syndrome (if the Eaters in Night didn't get them first). Not to mention the fact that the vain exhibitionists who compiled these tomes and grimoires, strung out between the narcissistic urge to self-exposure and their occupational addiction to secrecy, littered their scribbled recipes with booby traps on purpose, just to fuck with unauthorized imitators and prove how 'leet they were for being able to actually make this junk work without melting their own faces.

But the young idiot savant HPL was unaware of the social context of 18th century occultist fandom. So he naively distilled their methanol-contaminated moonshine and nonsense into a heady brew that makes you go blind and then causes your extremities to rot if you actually try to drink it. It's almost as if he mistook his grandfather's library for a harmless source of material for fiction, rather than the demented and dangerous documentation of our superstitious forerunners.

The Anarchist Cookbook, with its dangerously flawed bomb formulae, hasn't maimed half so many hands as HPL's mythos. His writings look more like fiction than allegorically-described recipes to most people, which is a good thing; but every so often a reader of his more recondite works becomes unhealthily obsessed with the idea of the starry wisdom behind it, starts thinking of it as something real, and then tries to reverse-engineer the design of the pipe bomb he's describing, not realizing that Quality Control was *not* his strong point.

There are bits of the True Knowledge scattered throughout HPL's oeuvre like corn kernels in a turd. But he left stuff out, and he added stuff in, and he embellished and added baroque twiddles and stylistic curlicues as only H. P. Lovecraft could, until it's pretty much the safest course to discount everything he talks about—like Old Bat-Wings himself, Dread Cthulhu, who dead but dreaming sleeps in Drowned R'lyeh beneath the southern ocean.

Watch my lips: Cthulhu does *not* exist! And there is no tooth fairy.

(Santa Claus is another matter; but that, as they say, is a file with a different code word...)

EAST GRINSTEAD IS buried deep in the heart of the Sussex commuter belt: this is Ruralshire, nor are we out of it. It's an overgrown village or a stunted town, depending on how you look at it, complete with picturesque mediaeval timbered buildings, although these days it's mostly known for its weirdly large array of fringe churches. I stumble blinking from the railway station (which is deathly quiet at this time of day, but clearly rebuilt to accommodate rush hour throngs), narrowly avoid being run down by a pair of mounted police officers who are exercising their gigantic cavalry chargers outside the station in preparation for crowd control at the next sudden-death derby (Brighton Wanderers v. Bexhill United, or some such), and hail a taxi. A minute's muttered negotiation with the driver ensues, then I'm off to the office.

When we arrive, I'm half-convinced I've got the wrong address. It's way the hell up the A22, so far out of town that at first I'm wondering why I got off the train in East Grinstead—but no, that's what Google said. (Not for the first time I wish I had a car, though as I live in London on a civil service salary it's not a terribly practical wish.) The taxi drops me in the middle of nowhere, next to a driveway fronted by a thick hedgerow. There are no obvious offices here, much less the sort of slightly fly-blown agricultural veterinary premises you'd expect the Animal Health Executive Agency to maintain. So I look around, at a loss for a minute until I notice the discreet sign pointing up the drive to the Equine Veterinary Practice.

I amble into the yard of what looks like a former farmhouse. It's been inexpertly fronted with a conservatory that houses a rather dingy reception area, complete with a bored-looking middle-aged lady tapping away on her computer while wearing an expression that says if it's MySpace, she's just been unfriended by the universe.

"Hello," I ask her. She ignores me, intently tapping away at whatever so preoccupies her on her computer. "Hello?" I repeat again. "I'm here to meet Mr. Scullery? Is he around?"

Finally she deigns to notice me. "He's on a job for the Department," she says. "He won't be available until Thursday—"

I let her see my teeth: "Perhaps you can tell him that Mr. Howard is here to see him? From the office in London. I assume it's the same job we're talking about."

"He's on a job for the—" Finally what I just said worms its way through her ears and into her brain—"I'm sorry, who did you say you were?"

"I'm Mr. Howard. I've come all the way down from London. About the Edgebaston brief." I bounce up and down on my toes. "He asked for me, so if you'd just like to—"

She is already reaching for the phone. "Hello? Mr. Scullery? I have a Mr. Howarth from London, he says you asked for someone from London to help with Edgebaston Farm? Is that right? Yes—right you are, I'll just tell him." She puts the phone down and smiles at me in that very precise, slightly self-deprecating way farm-bred ladies of a certain class use to let you know that there's nothing personal about the knee cap they're about to deliver to your left nut: "Mr. Scullery says he's running half an hour late and he'll be with you as soon as he can. So if you'd like to take a seat in the waiting area? I'm sure he won't be long." She turns back to her computer as if I'm invisible. I hover indecisively for a moment, but I know when I've been dismissed; and so I go and find a waiting room seat to occupy (sub-type: wooden, elderly, not designed with human buttocks in mind) and mooch listlessly through the stack of magazines for space aliens that they keep on hand to distract the terminally bored.

Dear Robert,

I must confess that, pursuant to my reply to your last missive, I experienced no small degree of self-doubt as to the perspicacity & pertinence of my critique. If you will permit me to attempt to justify my equivocation, I would like to enter in my defense a plea of temporary insanity. Your confabulation, while a most excellent evocation of a legendary monster, bears special & most unpleasant personal resonances from my regrettable youth. It is not your fault that the heraldic beast you chose to depict in this form is a marvelous horror in my eyes; indeed, you must be somewhat puzzled by my reaction.

I regret to inform you that your description of the unicorn, while vivid in its adhesion to the classical description of same & sharply piquant in depicting his pursuit of the gamine subject of the narrative, is fundamentally inaccurate in both broad outline & fine detail. Explorers might once have sketched fanciful depictions of the Chinese Panda, but today we are fettered by the dour tyranny of camera & zoo; to diverge so drastically from the established order of nature is to risk the gentle reader's willing suspension of disbelief.

Regrettably, the horrid creature you caricature is all too real; it will in due course be a matter of the most mundane familiarity to readers, & familiarity inevitably brings such enthusiastic flights of fancy as your missive to grief on the cold stone flags of reality.

Please extend me your trust on this matter. Unicorns are not a suitable topic for romance or fantasy. On the contrary, the adult unicorn is a thing of dire & eldritch horror & I would advise you to pray to your creator that you live to a ripe old age without once encountering such a monstrous creature.

I, alas, was not so lucky & the experience has blighted my entire adult life…

I kill time waiting for the Man from Ag and Fish by working my way through a stack of glossy magazines for aliens. Passing over the princess-shiny pinkness of *Unicorn School™: The Sparkling* with a shudder, I work my way through a thought-provoking if slightly breathless memoir of "Police Cavalry v. Pinko Commie Striking Miners in the 1980s"—the thoughts it provoke focus on the urgent need to commit the author to an asylum for the violently insane—and am partway through reading a feature about modern trends in castration techniques (and how to care for your gelding) in *Stallion World* when the door slams open and a gigantic beard wearing a loud tweed suit explodes into the reception area: "*Lissa!* Melissa! I'm back! Can you tell Bert to hose out the back of the Landy? And fetch out the two sacks of oats behind the passenger seat! Where's this man from the ministry? Ah, there you are! You must be Mr. Helmuth! I'm Greg Scullery. Pleased to meet you!"

He bounds across the reception area before I can put the magazine down and grabs my right hand, pumping it like a windlass while I'm still coming to my feet. Mr. Scullery is wiry and of indeterminate middle age. He could probably pass for a farmer with bizarre (albeit dated) sartorial taste—ghastly green tweed suit, check shirt, a tie that appears to be knitted from the intestines of long-dead badgers—but his beard is about thirty centimeters long, grizzled and salted and bifurcated. It has so much character that it's probably being hunted by a posse of typographers. "Um, the name's Howard. Bob Howard." I try not to wince at the sensation in my hand, which feels as if it has been sucked into some kind of machine for extracting oil from walnuts. "I believe you requested backup? For some sort of infestation?"

"*Yes!* Yes indeed!" I remember my other hand and use it to make a grab for my warrant card, because I have not yet had an opportunity to authenticate him.

"Seen one of these before?" I ask, flicking it open in front of him.

The walnut-crusher shifts gear into a final grind-into-mush setting: "Capital Laundry Services? Oh yes indeedy! I was in the Rifles, you know. Back in my misspent childhood, haha." The walnut slurry is ejected: my right hand dangles limply and I try not to wince conspicuously. "Jolly good, Mr. Howard. So. Have you been briefed?"

I shake my head, just as the bell above the reception area door jangles. A young filly is leading her mater in. They're both wearing green wellies, and there's something so indefinably horsey about them that I have to pinch myself and remember that were-ponies do not exist outside the pages of a certain best-selling kid-lit series. "Is there somewhere we can talk about this in private?" I ask Greg. "My manager said she didn't want to prejudice me by actually telling me what this is about."

His beard twitches indignantly while it sorts out an answer. "One of those, eh? We'll see about that!" He turns towards reception, where Jocasta or Penelope is trying to evince a metabolic reaction from Melissa the receptionist, who is still deep in MySpace meltdown. "Lissa! Belay all that, I'm going out on a job with Mr. Howard here! If Fiona calls, tell her I'll be back by five! Follow me." And with that, he strides back out into the farmyard. I swirl along in the undertow, wondering what I've let myself in for.

Greg leads me across the yard to a Land Rover. I don't know a lot about cars, but this one is pretty spartan, from the bare metal floor pan punctured by drain holes, to the snorkel-shaped exhaust bolted to one side of the windscreen. It's drab green, there's a gigantic spare tire clamped on the bonnet, and I wouldn't be surprised to hear it has an army service record longer than Greg's. That worthy clambers into the driver's seat and motions me towards the passenger door. "Yes, we have seat belts! And other modern fittings like air conditioning" (he points at a slotted metal grille under the windscreen), "and radio" (he gestures at a military-looking shortwave set bolted to the cab roof), "even though it's a pre-1983 Mark III model. Just hang on, eh?" He fires up the engine, which grumbles and mutters to itself as if chewing on lumps of coal, before it emits a villainous blue smoke ring as a prelude to turning over under its own power. Then he rams it into gear with a jolt, and we lurch towards the main road. I'm certain that the rubber band this thing uses in lieu of a leaf spring profoundly regrets how very, very wicked it was in an earlier life. And shortly thereafter, so do my buttocks.

Dear Robert,

Many thanks for your kind enquiry after my health. I am, as is usually the case, in somewhat precarious straits but no better or worse than is to be expected of a gentleman of refined & delicate breeding in this coarsened & debased age. My digestion is troubling me greatly, but I fear there is nothing to be done about that. I have the comfort of my memories, & that is both necessary & sufficient to the day, however questionable such comfort might be. I am in any event weighed down by an apprehension of my own mortality. The sands of my hourglass are running fast & I have no great expectation of a lengthy future stretching before me; so I hope you will indulge this old raconteur's discursive perambulations & allow me to tell you what I know of unicorns.

I should preface my remarks by cautioning you that I am no longer the young man whose memories I commit to paper. In the summer of 1904 I was a callow & untempered fourteen-year-old, with a head full of poetry & a muse at either shoulder, attending Hope High School & keenly absorbing the wisdom of my elders. That younger Howard was a sickly lad, but curious & keen, & took a most serious interest in matters astronomical & chymical. He was at heart an optimist, despite the death of his father from nervous exhaustion some years previously, & was gifted with the love of his mother & aunts & grandfather. Oh! The heart sickens with the dreadful knowledge of the horrid fate which came to blight my life & prospects thereafter. The death of my grandfather in that summer cast a pall across my life, for our circumstances were much reduced, & my mother & aunts were obliged to move to the house on Angell Street. I continued my studies & became particularly obsessed with the sky & stars, for it seemed to me that in the vastness of the cosmos lay the truest & purest object of study. It was my ambition to become an astronomer & to that end I bent my will.

There were distractions, of course. Of these, one of the most charming lived in a house on Waterman Street with her family & was by them named Hester, or Hetty. She attended Hope High, & I confess she was the brightest star in my firmament by 1908. Not that I found it easy then or now to speak of this to her, or to her shade, for she is as long dead as the first flush of a young man's love by middle age, & the apprehension of the creeping chill of the open grave that waits for me is all that can drive me to set my hand to write of my feelings in this manner. Far too many of the things I should have said to her (had I been mature enough to apprehend how serious an undertaking courtship must be) I whispered instead to my journal, disguised in the raiments of metaphor & verse.

Let me then speak plainly, as befits these chilly January days of 1937. Hetty was, Hetty was, like myself, the only child of an old Dutch lineage. A year younger than I, she brought a luminous self-confidence to all that she did, from piano to poetry. I watched from a distance, smitten with admiration for this delicate & clever creature. I imagined a life in literature, with her Virginia playing the muse to my Edgar & fancifully imagined that she might see in me some echoing spark of recognition of our shared destiny together. In hindsight my obsession was jejune & juvenile, the youthful obsession of a young man in whose sinews and fibers the sap is rising for the first time; but it was sincerely felt & as passionate as anything I had experienced at that time.

That was a simpler, more innocent age and there were scant opportunities for a youth such as I to directly address his muse, much less to plight his troth before the altar of providence & announce the depth of his ardor. It was simply not done. You may therefore imagine my surprise when, one stifling August Saturday afternoon, whilst engaged in my perambulations about the paths and churchyards of Providence, I encountered the object of my fascination crouching behind a gravestone, to all appearances preoccupied by an abnormally large & singular snail...

My tailbone is aching by the time Greg screeches to a halt outside a rustic-looking pub. "Lunch time!" He declares, with considerable lip-smacking; "I assume you haven't been swallowing the swill the railway trolley service sells? They serve a passable pint of Greene King IPA here, and there's a beer garden." The beard twitches skywards, as if reading the clouds for auguries of rain: "We'll probably be alone outside, which is good."

Mr. Scullery strides into the public bar (which is as countrified as I expected: blackened timber beams held together by a collection of mirror-polished horse brasses, a truly vile carpet, and chairs at tables set for food rather than serious drinking). "Brenda? Brenda! Ah, capital! That'll be two IPAs, the sausages and cheddar mash for me, and whatever Mr. Howard here is eating—"

I scan the menu hastily. "I'll have the cheeseburger, please," I say.

"We'll be in the garden," the beard announces, its points quivering in anticipation. And then he's off again, launching himself like a cannonball through a side door (half-glazed with tiny panes of warped glass thick enough to screen a public toilet), into a grassy back yard studded with outdoor tables, their wooden surfaces weathered silver-grey from long exposure. "Jolly good!" he declares, parking his backside on a bench seat with a good view of both the parking lot and the back door (and anyone else who ventures out this way). "Brenda will have our drinks along in a minute, and then we shall have a bite of lunch. So tell me, Mr. Howard. What *did* your boss tell you?"

"That you work for DEFRA and you know about us and you're cleared to request backup from my department." I shrug. "When I said she doesn't believe in prejudicing her staff I meant it. All I know is that I'm supposed to meet you and we're going to go and investigate a livery stable called, um,

G. Edgebaston Ltd. What's your job, normally? I mean, to have clearance—"

"I work for DEFRA in—" He pauses as a middle-aged lady bustles up to us with a tray supporting two nearly full beer glasses and some slops. "Thank you, Brenda!"

"Your food will be along in ten minutes, Mr. Scullery," she says with an oddly proprietorial tone; "don't you be overdoing it now!" Then she retreats, leaving us alone once more.

"Ah, where was I? Ah yes. I work for the Animal Health Agency." The beard twitches over its beer for a moment, dowsing for drowned wasps. "I'm a veterinary surgeon. I specialize in horses, but I do other stuff. It's a hobby, if you like, but it's official enough that I'm on the books as AHA's in-house crypto-zoologist. What about *you*, Mr. Howard? What exactly do you do for the Laundry?"

I am too busy trying not to choke on my beer to answer for a moment. "I don't think I'm allowed to talk about that," I finally manage. (My oath of office doesn't zap me for this admission.)

"Yes, but *really*, I say. What do you know about crypto-zoology?"

"Well." I think for a moment. "I used to subscribe to *Fortean Times*, but then I developed an allergy to things with too many tentacles…"

"Bah." Greg couldn't telegraph his disdain more clearly if he manifested a tiny thundercloud over his head, complete with lightning bolts. "Rank amateurs, conspiracy theorists and *journalists*." He takes a mouthful of the Greene King, filtering it on its way down his throat. "No, Mr. Howard, I don't deal with nonsense like Bigfoot or little grey aliens with rectal thermometers or chupacabra: I deal with *real* organisms, which simply happen to be rare."

"Unicorns?" I guess wildly.

Greg peers at me over the rim of his pint glass, one eye open wide. "Don't *say* that," he hisses. "Do you have *any* idea what we'd have to do if there was a unicorn outbreak in England? It'd make the last foot and mouth epidemic look like a storm in a tea-cup…"

"But I thought—" I pause. "Hang on, you're telling me that unicorns are real?"

He pauses for a few seconds, then wets his whistle before he speaks. "I've never seen one" he says quietly, "for which I am profoundly grateful because, being male, if I *did* see one it'd probably be the last thing I ever set eyes on. But I do assure you, young feller me lad, that unicorns are very real indeed, just like great white sharks and Ebola Zaire—and they're just as much of a joking matter. Napalm, Mr. Howard, napalm and scorched earth: that's the only language they understand. Sterilize it with fire and nerve gas, then station armed guards." Another mouthful of beer vanishes, clearly destined to fuel the growth of further facial foliage and calm Mr. Scullery's shaky nerves.

I shake my head. The EQUESTRIAN RED SIRLOIN dossier was suggestive, but it's always hard to tell where HPL's starry wisdom ends and his barking fantasy starts. "Okay, so you want backup when you go to run a spot check on Edgebaston's stable. Why me? Why not a full team of door-breakers, and a flame thrower for good luck?"

"They've got *connections*, Mr. Howard. Bob, isn't it? The Edgebastons have run Edgebaston Farm out at Howling ever since Harry Edgebaston married Dick and Elfine's daughter Sandra Hawk-Monitor, and renamed the old farm after his own line—and wasn't that a scandal, most of a century ago!—but in this generation they're pillars of the local community, not to mention the Conservative Club. Suppliers of horses to Sussex Constabulary, first cousins of our MP, Barry Starkadder. You do *not* want to mess with the squirearchy, even in this day and age of Euro-regulation and what-not. They'll call down fire and brimstone! And not just from the Church in Beershorn, I'm telling you. Questions will be asked *in Parliament* if I go banging on their front door without good reason, you mark my words!"

"But—" I stop and rewind, rephrasing: "something must have raised your suspicions, Mr. Scullery. Isn't that right? What makes you think there's an outbreak down at Edgebaston Farm?"

"I have a pricking in my thumbs and an itching in my nostril." The beard twitches grimly. "Oh yes indeed. But you asked the right question! It's the butcher bills, Mr. Howard, that got my attention this past month. See, old George has been buying in bulk from old Murther's butcher, lots of honeycomb and giblets and offal. Pigs' knuckles. That sort of thing. Wanda's happy enough to tell me what the Edgebastons are buying—without me leaning too hard, anyway—and it turns out they're taking about forty kilos a day."

"So they're buying lots of meat? Is that all?" I think for a moment. "Are they selling pies to Poland or something?"

"It's not food-grade for people, Mr. Howard. Or livestock for that matter, not since our little problem with BSE twenty years ago." Greg raises his glass and empties it down his throat. "And it's a blessed lot of meat. Enough to feed a tiger, or a pack of hounds, 'cept Georgie doesn't ride with the Howling Hounds any more. Had a falling-out with Debbie Checkbottom six years ago and that was the end of that—it's the talk of the village, that and Gareth Grissom wearing a dress and saying he wants a sex change, then taking off to Brighton." He says it with relish, and I try not to roll my eyes or pass comment on his parochial lack of savoir faire. This is rural England, after all; please set your watch back thirty years...

"Okay, so: meat. And a livery stable. Is that *all* you've got?" I push.

"No," Greg says tightly, and reaches into his pocket, pulls something out, and puts it on the table in front of me. It's the shell of a cone snail, fluted and spiraled, about ten centimeters long and two centimeters in diameter at its open end, gorgeously marbled in cream and brown. It's clearly dead. Which is a very good thing, because if it were a live cone snail and Greg had picked it up like that it would have stung him, and those bastards are nearly as lethal as a king cobra.

"Very nice," I say faintly. "Where did you find it?"

"On the verge of the road, under the fence at the side of the back field under Mockuncle Hill." The beard clenches, wrapping itself around a nasty grin. "It was alive at the time. Eating what was left of a lamb. Took a lot of killin'."

"But it's a—" I stop. I swallow, then realize I've got a pint of beer, and my dry throat really needs some lubrication. "It *could* be a coincidence," I say, trying to convince myself and failing.

"Do you really think that?" Greg knots his fingers through his beard and tugs, combing it crudely.

"Fuck, no." I somehow manage to make half a pint of beer disappear between sentences. "You're going to have to check it out. No question. In case there are females."

"No, Mr. Howard." He's abruptly as serious as a heart-attack. "*We* are going to have to check it out. Because if there's a live female, much less a mated pair, two of us stand a better chance of living long enough to sound the alarm than one..."

(cont'd.)

Having for so long been tongue-tied in her presence, I was finally shocked out of my diffidence when I saw the object of Hetty's interest. "I say, what is *that*?" I ejaculated.

My rosy-cheeked Dawn turned her face towards me & smiled like a goddess out of legend: "It is a daddy-snail!" she exclaimed. She reached towards a funerary urn wherein languished a bouquet of wilted lilies & plucked a browning stem from the funereal decoration—she was in truth poetry in motion. "Watch this," she commanded. My eyes turned to follow her gesture as she gracefully prodded the lichen-crusted rock before the snail's face. The shell of the snail was a fluted cone, perhaps eight inches long & two inches in diameter at the open end. Its color was that of antique ivory, piebald with attractive glossy brown spots. I could see nothing of the occupant & indeed it could have been a dead sea-shell of considerable size, but when the lily-stem brushed the gravestone an inch or two in front of it there was an excitement of motion: the cone rocked back on its heel & spat a pair of slippery iridescent tongues forth at the stem. With some disbelief I confess to recognizing these as *tentacles*, as unlike the foot of the common mollusk as can be (although our friends the marine biologists assert that the cephalopodia, the octopi & squid & chambered nautilus, are themselves but the highest form of invertebrate mollusk, so perhaps attributing ownership of tentacles to a land-snail is not such an incongruous stretch of imagination as one might at first consider); but while I was trying to make sense of my own eyes' vision, the demonic cone grabbed hold of the parched stem of the flower and *broke it in two*!

"Do you see?" Hetty beamed at me. "It is a daddy-snail!" Then her dear face fell. "But he is on his own, too far from home. There are no missy-horses here, & so he will surely starve & die unfulfilled."

"How do you know this?" I asked stupidly, confounded by her vivacity & veneer of wisdom in the matter of this desperate gastropod.

"I have a mummy-horse quartered in our stables," she told me, as matter-of-fact as can be, with an impatient toss of her golden locks. "Would you help me carry Peter back to the yard? I would be ever so grateful, & he would love to be among his kindred."

"Why don't you do it yourself?" I asked rudely, then kicked myself. Her speech and direct manner had quite confounded me, being as it was so utterly at odds with my imaginings of her lilting voice & ladylike gentility. (I was a young and dreamy boy in those days & so ill-acquainted with females as to picture them from afar as abstractions of femininity. It was a gentler & more innocent age &c., & I was a creature of that time.)

"I would, but I'm afraid he'd sting me," she said. "The sting of a daddy-snail is mortal harsh, so 'tis said."

"Really?" I leaned closer to see this prodigy for myself. "Who says?"

"Those families as raise the virgin missy-horses to ride or hunt," she replied. "Will you help me?" She asked with imploring eyes & prayerful hands, to such effect as only a thirteen-year-old girl can have on the heart-strings of a pigeon-chested boy of fourteen who has been watching her from afar and is eager to impress.

"Certainly I shall help!" I agreed, nodding violently. "But because it stings, I must take precautions. Would you wait here and stand vigilant watch over our escaped prisoner? I shall have to fetch suitable tools with which to fetter the suspect while we escort him back to jail."

She nodded her leave & I departed in haste, rushing up the lane towards home to borrow certain appurtenances from our own out-building. I fetched heavy gloves & fire-place tongs, the better with which to grasp a snake-tongued tentacular horror; and looking-glass, paper, & pencils with which to record it. Then I rushed back to the graveyard &

arrived quite out of breath to find Hetty waiting complaisantly near our target, who had moved perhaps a foot in the intervening quarter-hour.

I wasted no time at all in plucking the blasphemous mollusk from its stony plinth with tongs and gloves. As I lifted it, the creature stabbed out with a sharp red spike which protruded from the point of its shell: I was heartily glad for my foresight. "Where do you want me to take it?" I asked my muse. I gave the cone a sharp shake & the red spike retracted, sullen at being foiled.

Hetty clapped delightedly. "Follow me!" she sang, & skipped away between the gravestones.

Of course I knew the front of her parents' house on Waterman Street, but I felt it unwise to show any sign of this. I allowed Hetty to lead me through the boneyard & along a grassy path between ancient drystone walls to the alley abutting the back of her family home. There was a tall wooden gate, and beyond it a yard and stables. I was preoccupied with carrying the cone-shell at arm's length, for its homicidal rage had not escaped my attention. Periodically it shivered & shuddered, like a pot close to boiling over. Being thus distracted I perhaps paid insufficient attention to the warning signs: the flies, the evident lack of labour applied to cleaning the back stoop, & above all the sickly-sweet smell of rotting meat. "Come inside," Hetty said coyly, producing a key to the padlock that secured the gate. "Bring Peter with you!"

She opened the gate & nipped inside the yard. I followed, barely noticing as she secured the portal behind me with hasp & cunning padlock. "Come to the stable," she sang, dancing across the cobbles despite the pervasive miasma of decay that hung heavy over the yard like the fetid caul of loathsome exudate that hovers above the body of a week-dead whale bloating in Nantucket sound during the summer months. "Let me show you my darling, my one true love!" As she said it, the cone in my tongs gave a quiver, as of rage—or mortal terror. As it did so I gagged at the stench inside the yard, & my grip loosened inadvertently. The snail-thing gave another ferocious jerk, then slipped free! It caught the end of my tongs with one sucker-tipped tentacle, uncoiled to lower itself to the decaying straw-strewn cobbles below, then let go before I could respond. Hetty gave a little shriek of dismay: "Oh, the poor little man! Now the others will eat him alive!"

For what happened next I can only cite my callow youth & inexperience in exculpation. I panicked a little, tightening my grip on my tool as the deadly giant snail turned around as if assessing the arena in which it found itself. I took a step backwards. "What is going on?" I demanded.

The singular snail reared, point uppermost, as if tasting the sour & dreadful air. A host of small tentacles appeared around its open end, and it began to haul itself on suckers across the decay-slicked stones, proceeding in the direction of the stable doors & the darkness that I could even then sense lurking within.

Hetty smiled—a horrid, knowing expression, unfit to grace the visage of a member of the fairer sex. "The daddy-snails and the missy-horses dance together & dine, and those that survive join in matrimonial union to become a mummy-horse," she intoned in a sing-song way, as if reciting a nursery rhyme plucked from the cradles of hell. "*My* mummy-horse rests yonder," she said, gesturing at the decaying stable doors, slicked with nameless dark fluids that had been allowed to dry, staining the wood. "Would you like to see my mummy?"

I felt faint, for I knew even then that something terrible born of an unfathomable madness had happened here. Heartbroken—for there is no heartbreak like that of a fourteen-year-old lad whose muse reveals feet not of clay but of excrement—I nevertheless gathered my courage and stood my ground. "Your mummy," I said. "You do not speak of Mrs. van t'Hooft, in this case?"

She shook her head. "My *mother*—" she pronounced the word strangely—"is sleeping in the stable with mummy-horse. Would you like to see her?" A horrid glow of anticipation crept into her cheeks, as if she could barely conceal her eagerness to cozen me within.

I wound up the reins of my bravery to the breaking-point & tightened my grip on the fire-tongs. They felt flimsy & intangible in my grasp: oh for the shield and sword of a Knight of the Round Table! My kingdom for a charger & a lance, or even the cleansing flare of a dragon's hot breath! "Show me to your mummy-horse," I told Hetty, thinking myself brave & manly & willing to face down monsters for a young man's apprehension of love: thinking that whatever this monster was, I should have the better of it.

More fool I!

They do things differently in East Sussex, or so I gather. My informant in this matter is Greg Scullery, and the nature of the difference is a leisurely lunch at a country pub in place of a hasty sandwich break snatched at one's office desk in Central London.

I am initially worried about Greg's willingness to down a pint before lunch, but by the time our food arrives and we've cleaned our plates my worries evaporate—assisted by Greg's smooth transition onto lemonade and soda, albeit replaced by new worries about what we're going to find down on Edgebaston farm. Because Greg has got that disturbing snail-shell, and with the fresh context provided by the Lovecraftian confessional in the EQUESTRIAN RED SIRLOIN dossier, I'm going to have a hard time sleeping tonight unless I successfully lay that particular ghost to rest.

"It's not a horse, let's get that straight," Greg explains between bites of a disturbingly phallic sausage. "It's not *Equus ferus caballus*. It might *look* like one at certain points in its life cycle, but that's simple mimicry. Not Batesian mimicry, where a harmless organism imitates a toxic or venomous one to deter predators, much as hoverflies mimic the thoracic coloration of wasps, but rather the kind of mimicry a bolas spider uses to lure its prey—using pheromonal lures and appearance to make itself attractive to its next meal. It's an equoid not an equus, in other words."

I suppress a shudder. "How do you tell a female unic—equoid—from a real horse?" I ask.

"Come along to Edgebaston Farm and I'm sure I'll be able to show you," he says, setting aside the plate holding what's left of his bangers and mash as he rises to his feet. "Have you read the backgrounder I sent your people? Or the infestation control protocol?"

"All I've read is H. P. Lovecraft's deathbed confession," I admit.

"His—" Greg stops dead in his tracks—"*really?*"

"His first flame, Hetty van t'Hooft, introduced him to, well, he called it a unicorn. That was right before his nervous breakdown." I shake my head. "Although how much stock to place in his account…"

"Fascinating," Greg hisses between his teeth. "I bet he didn't mention napalm, did he?" I shake my head. "Typical of your effete word-pusher, then, *not practical*. But we can't just call in an air strike either, these days, can we? And it'll take rather a lot of pull to convince the police to take this seriously. So let's go and beard Georgina in her den and see what she's hiding."

I follow Greg through the pub and back to his Land Rover. "Are we just going to go in there and talk to her?" I ask.

"Because I thought uni—equoids—are a bit on the dangerous side? In terms of how they co-opt their host, I mean. If she's got a shotgun…"

"Don't you worry about Georgina, young feller me lad," Greg reassures me. "*Of course* she's got a shotgun! But she won't use it on us. The trick is to not look like we're a threat to her Precious, if she is indeed playing host to a fertile equoid. If we're lucky and she isn't under its spell things will go much more smoothly. So we're not going to mention the blessed thing at first. Remember she runs a farm? I'm just dropping in to check her hounds' vaccination records are up to date. While I'm doing that, you go and take a peek behind the stable doors with that phone camera of yours: then we'll put our heads together. Piece of cake!" he adds confidently, as he pushes the ignition button and his chariot belches blue smoke.

"Right." *You have got to be kidding*, I think, clinging to the grab bar for dear life as Greg shoves the Landy into gear and we bounce across ruts and into the road. "Do you have any idea of the layout of Edgebaston Farm? Because I don't!"

"It's jolly simple, Mr. Howard *sir*." (Oh great, now he's reverting to grizzled-veteran-sergeant-briefing-the-young-lieu-tenant mode.) "Edgebaston Farm covers two hundred acres on a hillside overlooking Howling, but the farm itself—the stables and outhouses—are in the shape of an octangle surrounding the farmhouse, which is a long triangle two stories high. The left point of the triangle, the kitchen, intersects the cowsheds which lie parallel to the barn, which is your target. They're all built from rough-hewn stone and thatched: no new-fangled solar panels here. It started out as a shed where Edward the Sixth housed his swineherds…"

"Yes, Greg, but what do I do if there's a fucking unicorn in the barn?"

"You run away very quickly, Bob. Or you die." He glances at me pityingly in the rearview mirror. (The Landy is sufficiently spartan that the reflector is an after-market bolt-on, with that imported American warning: *objects in mirror are closer than they appear*.) "Isn't that part of your job description? Screaming and running away?"

I am extremely dubious about my ability to outrun an equoid. "Uh-huh. The only kind of running I generally do is batch jobs on a mainframe." I clutch my briefcase protectively. "What we really need is a pretext to see what they're keeping in the stables, one that won't get us killed if you're right about what's lurking in the background." I pause for a moment. "They're a livery stable, aren't they? Do they do riding lessons?"

Greg nearly drives off the road. "Of course they do!" His beard emits an erratic hissing noise like a pressure cooker that's gearing up for a stove-top meltdown. After a moment I recognize it as something not unlike laughter. Eventually the snickering stops. "And if they're harboring equoids they won't be able to offer you a horse. But won't that take too long?"

"It had better not." I take a deep breath. "Okay, Greg. Here's our story: you're checking the dogs, and I'm your nephew from London. I'm working in Hastings for a month and while I'm there I want to learn to ride..."

How to describe the smell, the foulness, the louring portents of ominous doom that sent shivers of fear crawling up & down my spine? At the remove of a third of a century, that scene still retains the power to strike terror into my craven heart. I am no adventurer or chevalier; I am an aesthete & man of letters, ill-suited to the execution of such deeds. And though at fourteen I was in the flush of youth, and fancied myself as prepared for deeds of manly heroism

as any other lad, I yet held a shadowy apprehension of that
future self whom I was fated to become. I, Howard Phillips
Lovecraft Esq., a man of contemplative & refined sensibili-
ties born into a decadent latter age of feral brutes menaced by
the unspeakable stormclouds of Bolshevism & Jew-Fascist
Negro Barbarism sweeping the old countries of Europe, fear
that I am nothing more than a commentator, doomed to
write the epitaph to Western civilization that will, engraved
upon its stony headstone, inform the scholars of a future
age—should any eventually emerge from the imminent
darkness—of the cause of its fate.

People like my Hetty. People who with the best will
in the world would take in & nurture at their rosy breasts
the suckling horror that in my fictions I have named Shub-
Niggurath, the spawning goat of a thousand young, a
shuddering pile of protoplasmic horror that mindlessly cop-
ulates with itself and, spurting, squirting, licking its own
engorged & swollen *membrum* & *vulvae,* inseminates with
sucker-adorned tentacles (each cup enfolding the horror of
a barbed, venomous hook with which to tear the flesh to
which it adhered) the inflamed orifices & lubricious, pulsing cysts from which the abnormal spawn gushes in ropy
streams of hideous liquor—

Ia! How to describe the foul smell, the vile purulent
exudate of eldritch emulsion bearing gelatinous bubbles
of toadspawn from its body, did toadspawn only contain
minuscule conical snail-bodies & horse-like bodies—not
sea-horses yet, for no sea-horse has legs, but bodies *of the size
of* sea-horses—Ia! The language of the English lacks a suffi-
ciency of obscenity to encompass the monstrous presence of
Hetty's "mummy-horse." It looked at me with liquid brown
eyes as deep as any mare's, long-lashed & contemplative: some
of them embedded within it, others extruded atop stalks like
those of a vile unclean slug. It had mouths, too, and other

organs, some of them equine, others bizarrely, inappropriately human. I am reduced to the muttered imprecations of the subhuman & deranged; unmanned & maddened by the apprehension of the limits of sanity imposed by witnessing the ghastly immanence of an Elder Thing come to spawn in a family stable in Providence.

Imagine, if you will, a huge pile of gelatinous protoplasm ten feet in diameter & six feet high! It bears the charnel stink of the abattoir about it, a miasma composed of the concentrated fear & faecal vileness of every animal it has consumed to reach its present size. *Their* bones & skulls lie all around, & it is evident from a swift perusal of the scene that though it started on its equine stable-mates, the "mummy-horse," gracile & pallid, with the calcified body of a spiral coned snail fused to the bone between its eyes, has absorbed its own legs, & head, & indeed every portion of its anatomy not dedicated to its adult functions of eating & spawning. There are *human bones* scattered around the festering midden in which it nests, for its virginal bellwether has with girlish laughter & coy blandishments tempted first the human members of the household & then every adult she can reach to enter the den of the monster. It is the way of this horror that when she finally ceases to provide it with a banquet of men & women, boys, girls, & babies, it will take her for its final repast, & subsequently it too will succumb, for its cannibal kind feed their spawn not with milk but with their own suppurating, foul flesh.

I know not from which hadean pit of horrors the spawn of the unicorn hail, but through subsequent years of research I have learned this much: that the cone-snails are the male offspring & the "horses" are female, and they tear & bite & eat anything that approaches them except a member of the distaff sex. They mate not by insemination but by fusion, the male adhering to the forehead of the female. Their circulatory systems fuse & the male is presently absorbed, leaving behind a spiral-fluted horn containing only the reproductive gonads, which presently discharge via the shared venous circulation. Once mated, the tiny "unicorns" tear into the maternal corpus, bloating their stomachs & growing rapidly; they squabble over the remains & spear one another & cannibalize their weaker siblings, until in the end the survivors—barely two or three in each litter of thousands—leave their charnel nursery behind & set out in search of a new virgin hostess who will take them in & groom & feed them. And so the wheel of death rolls ever on...

There is cold comfort to be drawn from the sure and certain knowledge that the correct way to deal with the problem you're facing in your job involves napalm, if you find yourself confronting a dragon and you aren't even carrying a cigarette lighter.

(Thumps self upside the head: Dammit, HPL's style is infectious! Let me try again...)

With Greg driving me—if not mad, then at least in the direction of a neck brace—I barely notice either the time or the road layout as we hurtle towards Edgebaston Farm. We arrive all too soon at a desolate drystone wall overlooking a blasted heath, judder across a cattle grid set between the whitewashed gate posts, and embark on a hair-raising hillside descent along a poorly-maintained driveway that ends in a yard surrounded by mostly-windowless outbuildings that look like the mediaeval predecessors of World War II bunkers. It is not remotely like any of my preconceptions of what livery stables should look like—but then, what do I know?

Greg pulls up sharply and parks between a Subaru Forester covered in mud to the door sills and a white BMW. I do a double-take when I spot the concealed light-bar of an unmarked Police car on the BMW's rear parcel shelf. I remember what Greg said about the Edgebastons supplying the local cops with horses for their mounted police. Back home in London they're more interested in flying squirrels—Twin Squirrel helicopters, that is—but I guess here in Ruralshire they still believe in a cavalry charge with drawn batons and added eau de pepper spray. Or maybe the Chief Constable rides with the local Hunt. Either way, though, it's a warning to me to be careful what I say. In theory my warrant card is supposed to compel and command the full cooperation of any of HMG's servants. In practice, however, it's best to beware of local entanglements...

Greg marches up to the farmhouse door and is about to whack it with the knurled knob-end of his ash walking stick when it opens abruptly. The matronly lady holding the door handle stares at him, then suddenly smiles. "Greg!" she cries, not noticing me. I take stock: she's fortyish, about one-sixty high and perhaps seventy kilos, and wears jeans tucked into green wellies with a check shirt and a quilted body-warmer, as if she's just stepped in from the stables. Curly black hair, piercing blue eyes, and the kind of vaguely familiar facial bone structure that makes me wonder how many generations back it diverged from the royal family. "How remarkable! We were just talking about you. Who's this, are you taking on work-experience trainees?"

I emulate lockjaw in her general direction, it being less likely to give offense than my instinctive first response.

"Georgina," says Greg, "allow me to introduce my colleague—"

"Bob," I interrupt. Georgina darts forward, grabs my hand, and pumps it up and down while peering at my face as if she's wondering why water isn't gushing from my mouth. "From London." It's best to keep introductions like this as vague as possible.

"Bob," she echoes. To Greg: "Won't you come in? Inspector Dudley is here. We were discussing retirement planning for the mounted unit's horses."

"Jack Dudley's here, is he?" Greg mutters under his breath. "Capital! Come on, young feller me lad." And with that, he follows Georgina Edgebaston as she retreats into the cavernous farm kitchen. "And how is your mother, Georgie?" Greg booms.

"Oh, much the same—"

"—And where's young Lady Octavia?" Greg adds.

"Oh, she's back at school this week. Jolly hockey sticks and algebra, that kind of thing. Won't be back until half-term." The lady of the manse calls across the kitchen: "Inspector! We have visitors, I hope you don't mind?"

"Oh, not at all." A big guy with the build and nose of a sometime rugby player rises from the far end of the table, where he's been nursing a chipped mug. He's not in uniform, but there's something odd about his clothing that takes me a moment to recognize: boots and tight trousers with oddly placed seams, that's what it is. He's kitted out for riding, minus the hard hat. He nods at Greg, then scans me with the professional eyeball of one who spent years carrying a notepad. "Who's this?"

"Bob Howard." I smile vacuously and try not to show any sign of recognizing what he is. There's another guy at the far end of the kitchen, bent over a pile of dishes beside the sink. I get an indistinct impression of long, lank hair, a beard, and a miasma of depression hanging over him. "Greg's showing me around today. It's all a bit different, I must say!"

"Bob's a city boy," Greg explains, as if apologizing in advance for my cognitive impairment. "He's working in town for a month, so I thought I'd show him round. He's my sister's eldest. Does something funny with computers."

That's getting uncomfortably close to the truth, so I decide to embellish the cake before Greg puts his foot in it: "I'm in web design," I say artlessly. "Is that your car outside?" I ask Dudley.

The inspector eyeballs me again. "Company wheels," he says. To Georgina, he adds, "Well, I really should be going. Meanwhile, if you can think of anyone who has room to take in our retirees I'd be very grateful. It's a problem nobody mentioned in the original scope briefing—"

"A problem?" Greg asks brightly.

"Jack's looking for a new retirement farm for the Section's old mounts," Georgina explains. "We used to take them in here, but that's no longer possible."

"Old mounts?" I ask.

My obvious puzzlement gives them a clear target for a patronizing display of insider knowledge. "Police horses don't come cheap," Greg explains. "You can't put any old nag up against a bunch of rioters." (The inspector nods approvingly, as if Bexhill-upon-Sea might at any time to supply a riot whose average age is a day under seventy! Horses v. wheelchairs...) "They have to use larger breeds, and they have special training. And they don't stay in service forever—in at six, retired by sixteen. But that's relatively young to retire a horse, so the number of stables who can handle an ex-police mount is relatively small."

"We used to take them in until suitable new owners could be found," Georgina explains, "but that's out of the question now—we're at full occupancy. So I was just explaining to the inspector that while I can help him find a fallback, I can't take Rose and Oak when they reach retirement next month." She smiles politely. "Would you care for a cup of tea?"

"Don't mind if I do!" Greg chortles. I nod vigorously, and refrain from paying obvious attention as the inspector makes his apologies and slithers out of the kitchen. I'm a good boy;

I pretend I don't even notice him eyeballing the back of my neck thoughtfully from the doorway. Ten to one he'll be asking questions about me over Airwave before he gets back to the local nick. Let him: he won't learn anything.

"So why can't you take the police horses?" I ask as disingenuously as possible, while Georgina fusses over kettle and teapot. "Are you full or something?"

Greg spots my line of enquiry and provides distracting cover: "Yes, Georgina, what's changed?" he asks.

She sighs noisily. "We're out of room," she says. "Leastwise until we can empty the old woodshed out and get it ready to take livestock instead." She turns to the guy at the sink: "Adam, would you mind taking your clettering outside, there's a good lad? Mr. Scullery and I need a word in private."

Mr. Miasma rises and, wordlessly but with misshapen stick in hand, heads for the door. "I came to check the hounds' vaccination log book was up to date," Greg begins, "but if there's something else you'd like me to take a look at—"

"Well, actually there is," says Georgina. "it's about the stables." She's wringing her hands unconsciously, which immediately attracts my attention. "And those damned land snails! They're getting everywhere and I really can't be doing with them. Ghastly things! But it's mostly the new police mares. Jack convinced me to take them in for early training and breaking to saddle, but they've been an utter headache so far. "

"New mares," echoes Greg. I'm all agog, but as long as Greg is doing the digging I see no reason to interrupt. "What new mares would these be?"

Georgina sighs noisily again as she picks up the kettle and fills the teapot. "Sussex Police Authority's Mounted Police Unit, operating out of the stables in St. Leonards, is in the throes of phasing out all their medium-weight mounts and replacing them with what they call Enhanced-Mobility Operational Capability Upgrade Mounts, or EMOCUM—god-awful genetically engineered monstrosities, if you ask me, but what do I know about how the police work out their operational requirements?" She puts the kettle down, then dips a spoon in the teapot and gives it a vigorous stir. "So it's goodbye to Ash and Blossom and Buttercup, and hello to EMOCUM Units One and Two, and if it *looks* like a horse and *acts* like a horse—most of the time—then it's a horse, so it needs stabling and currying and worming and training, stands to reason; but if you'll pardon my French, this is *bullshit*. Unit Two tried to eat Arsenic, so I have to move him out of the stable—"

"What? When was that? Why didn't you call me?" demands Greg. His beard is quivering with indignation.

Georgina rolls her eyes, then opens a cabinet and hauls out a double handful of chipped ceramic mugs. "You were attending to a breech delivery, one of old Godmanchester's Frisians as I recall. Melissa sent Babs instead and she patched him up—"

"Why would you leave arsenic lying around in a stable?" I ask, finally unable to contain myself. "Isn't that a bit risky?"

Two heads swivel as one to regard the alien interloper. "Arsenic is Octavia's horse," Georgina explains, her voice slow and patient. "A seventeen-year-old bay gelding. He used to belong to Jack's mounted unit but they put him out to pasture two years ago. Sixteen-and-a-half hands, police-trained, perfect for an ambitious thirteen-year-old."

I'm blinking at this point. I recognize "police," but the rest of the words might as well be rocket science or motorbike internals for all I can tell. All I can work out is the context. "So he's a horse, and he was attacked by one of these EMOCUM things?" I ask. "Was that serious?"

"It tried to *eat* him!" Georgina snaps. I recoil involuntarily. "It has *canines*! You can't tell me that's natural! It's messing with the natural order of things, that's what it is. Amos was right." She gives the tea another violent stir, then sloshes a stream of orange-brown liquor into the mugs—one of those breakfast blends with more caffeine than espresso and a worrying tendency to corrode stainless steel—and shoves them at Greg and myself. (Americans think we Brits drink tea because we're polite and genteel or something, whereas we really drink it because it's a stimulant and it's hot enough to sterilize cholera bacteria.) I accept the mug with some trepidation, but it doesn't smell of sheep-dip and my protective ward doesn't sting me, so it's probably not a lethal dose. "Babs stitched him up, but we can't get him to go anywhere near the stable now—he panics and tries to bolt."

"Where are you keeping him for the time being?" Greg asks, with the kindly but direct tone of a magistrate enquiring after the fate of a mugger's victim.

"He's in the south paddock while I sort out getting the woodshed refitted as a temporary stable, but there's damp rot in the roof beams. And we had to move Travail and Jug-Jug, too. Not to mention Graceless, Pointless, Feckless and Aimless, who are all under-producing and their milk is sour and they won't go anywhere near the yard. It's a disaster, except for the cost-plus contract to look after the new Units. An absolute disaster! For two shillings I'd sell them to a traveling knacker just to get rid of them. But that'd leave Jack in the lurch, and the police with nowhere to put the other six they've got coming, and we can't be having that, so think of England, say I."

Greg takes a swig of rust-colored caffeine delivery fluid: the beard clenches briefly around it, then swallows. "Well, I suppose we'd better take a look at these EMOCUM beasties. What do you think, young feller?"

"I think that'd be a very good idea," I say cautiously. My head's spinning: Georgina has swapped out the game board from underneath our original plan—and what the *hell* are the police playing at? "Then I think we'd better go and have a word with Inspector Dudley. I have some questions for him, starting with where he got the idea of re-equipping the mounted unit with equoids..."

To paraphrase the stern & terrible Oliver, I beseech you, Robert, in the bowels of Christ, think it possible that you may be mistaken about unicorns. They are an antique horror that surpasses human understanding, a nightmarish reminder that we are but swimmers in the sunlit upper waters of an abyss & beneath us in the inky darkness there move monsters that, though outwardly of fair visage, harbor appetites less wholesome than Sawney Bean's. As Professor Watts reminds us, fully three-quarters of life's great & bounteous cornucopia consists of parasites, battening furtively on the flesh of the few productive species that grace creation. It is true that some of these parasites are marvelously attuned to the blind spots of their hosts; consider the humble cuckoo & the way its eggs, so different in shape & color from those that surround them, are nevertheless invisible to the host that raises the changeling in the nest. Just so too do unicorns exploit our beliefs, our mythology, our affection for our loyal equine servants! But their fair visage is merely a hollow mask that conceals a nightmare's skull.

I knew none of that as I stood in that terrible courtyard, feet braced uncertainly on slime-trailed cobblestones slick with the mucilaginous secretions of the flesh-eating snails, facing the darkness within the gaping jaws of the stable with only a pair of steel tongs in my hand—and the looking-glass I had fetched with some vague, childish idea of sketching the details of the snail's shell to compare with the encyclopedia in my grandfather's library. Standing there in that revelatory moment of which I have dreamed ever since, I knew only Hetty's blasphemous grin, the slithering horror of the tentacular mollusk as it fled towards the stables, and an apprehension of the greater nightmare that lurked beyond that shadow'd threshold.

But I was not unarmed! A stack of chopped lumber lay beneath a roof at one side of the barn, & the yard was strewn with moldering hay. I strode across, trying not to look within those horrid doors, & seized a slender branch that had been left intact, presumably as kindling.

"What are you doing?" demanded Hetty: "Won't you go inside right away? Mummy-horse needs help!"

"It's all right," I consoled her; "but I need to see what I'm doing if I am to help her." And with that facile reassurance I scooped up a handful of straw & used my handkerchief to bind it around the stick. Then I strode to the sunlit corner of the yard & pulled out my glass, bringing it to a focus on the straw.

Hetty stared at me oddly, then retreated to the barn door, her hips swaying lasciviously as she beckoned. There was, I recall, a sultry smile on her lips & a glazed & lustful expression that I, in my juvenile naïveté, barely apprehended was contrived to be seductive. As she stepped backwards into the shadows she raised her petticoats, revealing far more leg than common decency normally allowed in those days. I shuddered. "Won't you come with me?" she sang.

The tip of my wand erupted with a pale glow. I breathed on the straw until it caught. I found myself wishing I had some tar or paraffin; with barely a minute until it burned down, I knew I had scant opportunity. I stepped toward her, a steely resolve in my chest propelling me forward even though my knees nearly knocked together & my teeth clattered in my head. "I'm coming, dear," I said as Hetty retreated further into darkness, lifting her dress over her hips. She wore—pardon me for the nature of this confession—nothing beneath it, but was naked as the day she was born. Livid bruises studded her pale thighs, some of them circular, with puncture marks at their centers, scabbed-over wounds that hinted at unholy practices. No dance of the seven veils was this, but rather the puppet-show of a diseased and depraved imagination, seeking to corrupt & abuse the feeble-minded & weak-willed & lure them to a fate of unspeakable moral degeneracy.

The choking air within the barn reeked of overpowering decay, tempered by a musky odor that set my loins aflame despite my terror. I saw a lamp hanging from a nail just inside the door. Seizing it, I hastily applied the torch (fading to embers even then) to the wick, and just in time: for it caught. I raised the lamp & wound the wick up until it flared, & forced myself to look past Hetty—shamefully naked now, thrusting her hips towards me & supporting her uncorseted bosom with both hands in a manner transparently calculated to attract my attention—to behold the benthic horror of the angler fish lurking half-unseen in the twilight, dangling its shapely lure before me—its chosen prey!

This abomination stared at me with those glistening, liquid horse-eyes & woman-eyes: and it repeatedly coiled & recoiled tentacles like those of the Pacific octopus. Mouths opened & closed as those muscular ropes twitched & slithered around Hetty's feet. "Do you want me?" her sweet soprano offered, even as a pink-skinned tentacle with fewer suckers than most spiraled around her left leg, questing & climbing. "Mummy-horse says don't be afraid!" The pink & blindly questing *membrum* passed the level of her knees. "Mummy says she would like to speak with you, in a minute, through my mouth—" The tentacle's blind head (the *hectocotylus*, as I later identified it) reached between her buttocks from behind. Pulses shivered up it from stem to tip as she opened her cloacal passage to receive it with a sigh. Her knees flexed towards me, baring her naked womanhood, as her weight collapsed onto that vile and corrupt pillar of muscle. It supported her fully: her eyes rolled back in her head as she fainted. *"Howard,"* said another's voice, speaking through her throat. *"Come to me & join in precious union with this mating body, for your arrival has been prophesied by the ancients of our kind & you will be a fitting adornment to my reign."*

"Wh-what are you?" I asked, mesmerized—I was, as I have said, but a youth: I had never seen a woman's secret parts before, & even in the midst of this terrible *wrongness* I was excited as well as afraid—for it did not occur to me then that my very soul was in immediate danger.

"We are Shub-Niggurath," said the cyclopean nightmare that spoke through Hetty's vocal cords; *"we come from your future & it is prophesied that you will become one with our flesh."*

Hetty's body now began to rise, legs straightening. Her arms rose too, outstretched and imploring towards me. Her neck righted itself & her eyes opened. "Howard?" she said in her normal voice. Then in the voice of Shub-Niggurath: *"Mate with us & give us the gift of your seed."* Then again: "Howard? Something is wrong! I'm afraid..."

I stepped closer, mesmerized. Then another step. By the light of my raised oil lamp I beheld tears of blood weeping from her eyes. By my every inhalation I could perceive (from among the overwhelming, choking midden-stink of the stables) a peculiar stench emanating from her skin in place of the normal fragrance of the fairer sex. "Isn't this your mummy-horse?" I asked, driven by a cruel impulse: I wanted to touch her, I wanted to open myself to experiences I as yet had no understanding of: powerful emotions drove me on, no longer pure and holy terror but now tempered with an admixture of feral lust. "Isn't *this* what you want?"

"She hasn't done this to me before—" Shub-Niggurath: *"Take the gift we place before you, boy. Lose yourself in the flesh of Hetty van t'Hooft & revel in the pleasure & ecstasy of the union of bodies & souls! Join us, join us, join us!*" I saw the thick column of cephalopodian flesh pulsing behind & within her, operating her skin like a hellish glove puppet, & I slowly realized: this thing, this hideous monster that spawned endlessly in the filthy darkness of the family stable, was *hollowing her out from the inside*! It meant to use her as a lure, just as the angler mercilessly impales a fly on a barbed hook—& I was the juicy trout in its sights! The musky scent hanging all around made my heart beat faster & brought premature life to my youthful manhood, but *even then* I recognized that to succumb to such an unholy lust was a mistake I could ill afford to make.

Even so, I took another step forward. It was to nearly prove my undoing, for I had paid scant attention to the spawn that surrounded us, lurking in the far corners of the barn. But the spawn had begun to close in, ready to resume tearing at the flesh of their progenitor, and now by pure mischance I brought my shod foot down on an over-eager unicorn. It was a perfect miniature pony perhaps a hand high at the hock, sporting a viciously sharp horn an inch long. It screamed in a high-pitched voice & I slipped, falling to one knee. I looked up, straight at Hetty's female parts, & saw then what had been hidden in waiting for me: a livid appendage, either vastly expanded from her natural organ (like the *clitoris* of the spotted hyena) or worse, an extrusion of Shub-Niggurath itself, capped with the concentric circular jaws of a lamprey, alternately gaping open to bite & snapping closed with vile frustration, streaked with blood & mucus, pulsing as it quested blindly from its vulval nest to seek my face—

I screamed & threw the oil lamp. Then I pushed myself to my feet & fled. Fiery stabbing pain lanced through my hand; I glanced down & saw that I had been stung by the

lance of a small snail-cone. The agony was pure & excru-
ciating, & as breathtaking as a hornet sting. I caught my
breath & screamed again, then stumbled backwards. Hetty
was still upright, but quivered from head to toe in a quite
inhuman manner, which I now know to be death spasms,
like those that are seen when a felon is being hanged. Blood
trickled from the sides of her mouth & from her ears now, as
well as from the sides of her twitching eyes. The vileness that
supported her skin now ate at her innards with its concealed
radulae. But even as it consumed her & tried to extend its
tentacles towards me, the spreading pool of oil from the
lamp reached a half-collapsed bale of hay that lay beside a
bloody exposed rib cage (whether of man or beast I could not
tell, in the depths of my torment).

"We will be back," the horror gurgled through her dying
larynx: *"and we will have you in the end!"*

The flames caught as I stumbled away, cradling my
burning, wounded hand. I remember naught of the next two
weeks but nightmares, but I was later told I lay febrile &
unconscious & shuddering on the edge of death's dark cliff.
Thereafter, whenever I was introduced to a member of the
fairer sex who might flirt with me or whisper sweet noth-
ings, all I could see was the husk of my Hetty, impaled and
half-eaten on the tentacle of a nightmare from the far future,
even as she whispered chilling blandishments to me; and all I
could think of was the thing that lay in wait for me, & what
the Beast had said at the end.

Not until I met the blessed Sonia was I was even partially healed of the wound in my soul that the *unicorn*
inflicted. Even today I am only half the man that I might
have been had I not met the abomination in the stable. And
this is why I urge you not to write lightly of the four-legged
parasite that preys upon our instinct to protect & cherish
the fairer sex. They are a thing of unclean & blasphemous

appetites that preys upon the weak & foolish & our own intrinsic tendency towards degeneracy & self-abuse. Worse still, they harbor a feral intellect *and they plan ahead.* They *must* be destroyed on sight! Otherwise the madness & horror will breed, until only darkness remains.

After we drain our mugs of tea, Georgina shepherds us out into the farmyard to show us Lovecraft's Nightmares: Police Rapid Pursuit Edition.

I am actually quite apprehensive at this point, you understand. I've read enough of old purple-prose's deathbed confessions to Robert Bloch to be aware that unicorns are very unpleasant indeed. Even making allowances for Hipster Lovecraft's tendency towards grisly gynophobic ranting, Freudian fever-fantasies, and florid exaggeration, we're clearly about to meet something deeply creepy. Greg, for his part, is suitably subdued: even his beard hangs heavy, as if it senses a thunderstorm-drenching in the offing.

Only Georgina carries on as if everything is normal, and she at least has had time to get accustomed to the idea that there might be something nasty in one of the outbuildings. (Or standing next to the woodshed in a blanket with police high-visibility markings and a baton slung from the saddle. Whatever.) Also, Georgina has an ace up her sleeve— or maybe a baronetcy. She's clearly of such rarefied breeding that she feels no need to take shit from *anyone.* If you live in Ruralshire, England, you meet people like this from time to time. Their blood runs blue with self-confidence. Where ordinary folks enjoy messing around with flower beds, these folks open their garden to the Queen one weekend a year. The garden in question is probably one that their sixteen-times-great grandfather received as grace and favor after unhorsing an uppity duke during some battle everyone except mediaeval historians have forgotten about. If you catch them ranting about immigrants, chances are they're talking about those *nouveaux-arrivistes*, the Windsors. They dress in patched jeans, cable-knit sweaters, and green wellington boots; drive muddy Subarus or Land Rovers; own entire counties; and reduce police superintendents and MPs to helpless displays of forelock-tugging obeisance via some kind of weird reality distortion field.

Which probably makes Georgina the ideal person to look after a couple of fractious, under-trained, EMOCUM Units: because she takes no shit from anyone or anything, parasitic alien horrors from beyond spacetime included.

"I say! You there! EMOCUM Unit One! Stop trying to eat the vet *at once*! It's rude!"

A stable is a stable is a stable, except when, instead of regular horses, it contains carnivorous Furies with glowing blue eyes—in which case, the wooden partitions are reinforced with welded steel tubes, the brightwork on the bridles is made of machined titanium, and it stinks like the carnivore enclosure at a zoo where they've been feeding the lions and tigers rotten offal laced with laxatives. The stench when Georgina opens the side door makes my stomach heave, and I have to stand outside and take a few deep breaths before I can dive into the miasma. Suddenly the legend of the labors of Hercules—and the cleaning of the Augean stables—makes perfect sense to me.

When I manage to get my rebellious gastrointestinal tract under control, I step into a scene worthy of a Hieronymus Bosch triptych. It's like a stable, only reinforced, and equipped with devices that might in any other context be taken as instruments of torture, or at least evidence for the prosecution in a really serious animal abuse case: heavy shackles chained to concrete pillars, buckets of bloody intestines surrounded by clouds of buzzing flies, the omnipresent stench, humming fans and fluorescent lights. There are two horses present, one of whom appears to be leaning over the side of his stall and nibbling on Greg's beard with intent to be over-familiar, if Greg's indignant whimpering is taken into account. But then they notice my arrival. Both heads turn to focus on me. And I freeze, because they're not horses.

Being the object of attention of a pair of equoids—pardon me, Police EMOCUM Units—is a chilling experience. Have you ever been to a zoo or wildlife sanctuary and attracted the attention of a lion, tiger, or other big cat? You'll know what I'm talking about. Except equoids are horse-sized: two or three times as heavy as a (thankfully extinct) saber-toothed *Smilodon*, four times the weight of a modern Bengal tiger. They aren't quite in maximum-size Tyrannosaur territory, but they're not far off, and they're hot-blooded carnivores. When they focus on you, you simply *know* that they're wondering how you'll taste. It's a shuddery sensation deep in your gut that makes your balls try to climb up into your belly and hide (if you're male), and your ringpiece contract (regardless of sex). As they look at me I freeze and break out in a cold fear-sweat. They freeze too, heads pointing at me like gun muzzles.

Lots of details come into focus: they have no horns. Their eyes are slightly too close together, moved frontally to give them better binocular vision than any normal horse. Their nostrils and mouths look normal at first, but then one of them wrinkles its lips and I see fangs, and the edges of the lips retract much further than is natural for a grass-eater, revealing dentition more like something out of a nightmare concocted by H. R. Giger than anything a horse doctor might recognize. Oh, and the eyes? I mentioned that they're blue, and they pulse, but did I remember to say that they *glow*?

Resting on a stand next to one of the stalls is what passes for a saddle—one with a steel roll cage with wire mesh front and sides, and a police light bar on the roof. Obviously, riding an EMOCUM Unit is not a happy-fun experience. In point of fact, they exude danger so strongly that I'm wondering why the police didn't ask the saddlery to add machine gun mounts to the rider's safety cage—it couldn't be any less subtle.

"Who the fuck are they planning on deploying these things against?" I ask hoarsely; "An invading Panzer division?" Visions of the carnage after Dudley deploys his EMOCUMs for crowd control at a friendly away match overload even my normally-overactive sense of humor. These beasts are no laughing matter: you don't mock a main battle tank, either.

"*Grrrrr...*" rumbles equoid number one, inquisitively sizing me up for elevenses.

"I can't be sure," Georgina says thoughtfully, "but if I had to guess, I'd say they'll come in right handy when the illegal immigrants and bloody hippies in Brighton rise up to burn all us right-thinking people down. But in the meantime, they manufacture a hundred pounds of shit every day, and I can't even compost it!"

"Bastards," Greg mumbles indistinctly, clutching his chin.

"*Do* pay attention, I told you not to stand too close!" Georgina shakes her head. "They were a lot smaller when Jack dropped them off," she adds. She bends down, indicating knee height. "Still vicious as a bear-baiting dog, but at least they were manageable then."

"How long ago was that?" I ask, getting an even worse sinking feeling.

"About three weeks ago. They grow *fast*."

MINISTRY OF DEFENCE
SECRET
Procurement Specification: M/CW/20954

Date of Issue: July 1st, 1940

Requirement for:

Charger, Heavy Cavalry Mounted:

Must replace existing mounts for Horse Guards and other remaining Army Cavalry operational units.

Mounts should be between 13 and 17 hands high, weight 650–900 lbs, broken to saddle.

Desirable characteristics:

Mounts should exhibit three or more of the following traits:

- Endurance in excess of 6 hours at 30 miles/hour over rough terrain (when ridden with standard issue saddle, rider, and kit)
- Endurance in excess of 30 minutes at 50 miles/hour on metaled road surfaces (when ridden with standard issue saddle, rider, and kit)
- Ability to see in the dark
- Ability to recognize and obey a controlled vocabulary of at least 20 distinct commands
- Invisible
- Bulletproof
- Carnivorous
- Flight (when ridden with standard issue saddle, rider, and kit)

State of requirement:

Unfilled

CANCELLED April 2nd, 1945

Reasons for cancellation:

(1) Impending replacement of horse-mounted cavalry in all future operational roles,

(2) Procurement and initial delivery of AEC Centurion Mk 1 Universal Battle Tank supersedes requirement M/CW/20954.

Sitting back in the passenger seat of Greg's Landy, I massage my head as if I can somehow squeeze the aching contents into a semblance of order. "That was *not* what I was expecting."

"I've known Georgina since she was a wee thing, competing in dressage." Greg huffs for a moment, then produces a pencil case from the pile of debris under the driver's seat. He extracts what I initially mistake for a gigantic brown spliff. Then he produces a weird multitool, with which he amputates one end, and sets fire to the stump of the reeking roll-up.

"Careful with that spliff, Eugene," I start before I realize that it's actually a cigar, so old and foul that I cough up half a lung before I get the door open and scramble out. "Jesus, Greg!"

"Sorry, young feller." He's clearly unrepentant, but I notice that he's sucking on it like it's an asthma inhaler, and his other hand—the one grasping his walking stick—is shaking slightly. "I needs my weed after witnessing a scene like that."

"I am going to report this," I say heavily. "The EMOCUMs, I mean. This is *way* above my pay grade."

"Oh, really? I have never in all my days seen one of you people back down from a red-eyed abomination with too many tentacles—"

"You've never seen us pick a fight with the police, either, have you?" I snap at him, then walk it back: "Sorry, but we work *with* the boys in blue, they're not normally the subject of our investigations." I cough, trying to clear my lungs. They've been taking a battering today, between the fetid aroma of carnivore shit in the stables and Greg's diesel-smoked stogie. "Let me think. Okay, the EMOCUMs aren't going anywhere right now. They can wait for backup." (Assuming they're not actually one of *our* projects— one that Iris and I don't know about because we're not cleared for it. Crazier things have happened. In which case double-checking everything discreetly is the order of the day.) "But, hmm. What do you know about Inspector Dudley? Because he's the next link in the chain back to wherever they came from..."

The beard shakes like a bush in a hail-storm. "Sorry, lad, I can't help you. I deal with the likes of Georgina, or Sergeant Irving who runs the station stables in East Grinstead, not the organ grinder hisself."

"Who was conveniently present when we came to visit, and then slipped out. Oh *shit*."

"What's the matter?" Greg takes another epic lungful of vaporized bunker fuel, then his eyes wrinkle up. "You don't think—"

"When you sent a memo requesting a liaison visit from Capital Laundry Services, how exactly did you go about it?" I ask. "Did you by any chance ask someone else to send us an email? Someone like—"

"Gosh, now that you mention it—" He jabs his fingers knuckle-deep into his beard and tugs—"I'd ha' asked the fragrant Melissa to write to you! But I don't see—"

I roll my eyes. "Does Melissa have a boyfriend, by any chance?" I ask. "Who might happen to be a member of the local constabulary? Or a father or mother or sister or best pal from her school days, or something? Someone who might know about the EMOCUM procurement program?"

"Ooh, I see where you're going." Greg sighs, then reaches down and stubs out his vile cigar on the underside of his boot. He bags up the remains: I shudder slightly and climb back into the Land Rover's passenger seat. My stunned nasal passages can't make any sense out of their environment, but my pupils dilate and my pulse slows thanks to all the nicotine hanging in the air. "You're wondering where it all came from?"

"That's the key question," I agree, fastening my seat belt and pulling the door closed. "Where did Jack Dudley procure a handful of juvenile unfertilized female unicorns? And who put the idea into his head? Come to think of it, where are those bloody snails coming from? There's got to be a fertilized female in the sessile spawning phase of its life cycle somewhere hereabouts. It's one thing for some idiot mounted police officers to think that Baba Yaga's herd will be good for crowd control duty, but if there's any leakage—"

"I've got an inkling, but you're not going to like it. This could be the start of a large-scale outbreak," Greg says heavily. "A full infestation. Equoids are *r*-strategy spawners—" he catches my blank look and backs up. "Most organisms follow one of two types of reproductive strategy, young feller. *K*-selection—few offspring, lots of energy devoted to keeping them alive: that'd be us shaved apes, heh. And then there's *r*-selection: spew out thousands or millions of tiny spawn and hope some of them survive. Equoids do that, they spawn like pollen, or flies, or frogs... but they're also parasites that co-opt a host species and use it to nurture their brood. Anyway, the things in the barn, the adult sterile females, they're *unusual*. And that's a warning flag. If I had ter guess what's going on I'd figure there's a breeding queen out there who's worked out a low-cost way to help her spawn make it to adulthood. Something *new*, not just a single hypnotized girlie. Not sure what, but if we don't find the queen in time we're going to be neck deep in unicorns in these parts." He trails off into a grim and thoughtful silence.

"I'm going to phone home for support," I say. "Then while they're getting the circus loaded, I'll go pay the inspector a visit. I want to establish the facts on the ground, find out where he's getting the horses from."

"And what then? If you can't figure it out?"

"Whatever I find, I'm going to boot it upstairs then take a back seat. Like I said, this is well above my pay grade..."

I'M FAIRLY SURE that by this point in my report, you, gentle reader, will doubtless be raising a metaphorical hand, because the questions have been piling up thick and fast and you are reaching the end of your patience. So let me try to set your mind at ease with a quick run through the list of Frequently Asked Questions:

Q: Unicorns? Are they *really* this bad?

A: Yes. I wish I was making this up. Unfortunately old HPL's experience in his childhood sweetheart's back yard is about par for the course where those creatures are concerned. We are not in *Unicorn School™: The Sparkling* territory here. Or even *My Little Pony*. (Well, except for the Magic bit.)

Q: But what about the unfertilized ones?

A: It's the parasitic life cycle in a nutshell. Parasites, especially those with complex gender dimorphism and hypercastrating behavior (that diverts a host species' reproductive energies in service to their own goals) generally have some interesting failure modes. Among unicorns, if they don't mate young they tend not to mate at all—it's kind of hard for a foot-long cone snail to climb onto the forehead of something that resembles a carnivorous horse, isn't it? Especially without getting eaten. So the female grows to adult stature but is infertile. What you get is an equoid: an obligate meat-eater the size and shape of a horse, with the appetite of three Bengal tigers and the table manners of a hungry great white shark.

Q: Why haven't I heard about these already?

A: You probably have. There are plenty of legends about them—the mares of Diomedes, the Karkadann of Al-Biruni, the herd of Baba Yaga—but they don't show up very often in the historic record. This is because people who try to domesticate mature equoids usually end up as equoid droppings.

Q: But what if you get them young?

A: Good thinking! If you get them young you can semi-domesticate them. But to get them young, one has to locate a fertile adult in the sessile, spawning phase. (And survive the experience.)

Q: What are we supposed to do about them?

A: The sterile adult equoids themselves aren't necessarily a problem: they're basically dangerous but dumb. Georgina Edgebaston has been training two of them as EMOCUM Units, but they're under control. As long as she doesn't do anything stupid, like hitting one on the forehead with a *giant venomous land snail*, she's probably got them contained. I'm much more worried about where they're coming from. Equoids don't generally gambol freely on the Southern downs, because the trail of half-eaten children and screaming parents tends to attract attention. This means that there's probably a nest not too far away. And it is absolutely essential that Greg and I locate the nest so that it can be dealt with appropriately.

Q: The nest—what does "appropriate" mean in this context?

A: Let me give you a clue: I start by making some phone calls which, by way of a liaison officer or two, induce the police to evacuate the surrounding area. Then what appears to be a Fire Brigade Major Incident Mobile Command HQ vehicle arrives, followed by a couple of pumps which are equipped to spray something rather more toxic and inflammable than water. Finally, the insurance loss adjusters turn up.

That's what is supposed to happen, anyway. If it doesn't, Plan B calls for the Army to loan us a couple of Apache Longbow helicopter gunships. But we try not to go there; it's difficult and expensive to cover up an air strike, and embarrassing to have to admit that Plan A didn't work properly.

Q: You said equoids aren't intelligent. But what was all that Yog-Sothoth stuff HPL was gibbering about at the end? What about the mummy-thing—

A: Don't you worry your little head about that, it's above your security clearance. Just take it from me that everything is under control!

AFTER I PHONE Iris, to deliver the unwelcome news that this smoke appears to be associated with an ignition source, I continue my investigation by going in search of the inspector.

There is an old Victorian police station in East Grinstead, complete with the antique blue gas lamp over the main entrance and a transom window (no longer used) just inside the lobby door. It also has a pair of tall gates that open into a courtyard. It currently does duty as a car park for the uniform cars and snatch vans, but one wall of the courtyard is still lined with stalls for the horses, and they're in good repair.

I am a civilian, casually dressed. I do not enter the courtyard, but instead walk up to the public entrance, past the information posters (COPPER THEFT: ARE YOU TAKING YOUR LIFE IN YOUR HANDS?), and in to the reception area.

I stand in front of the desk for almost a minute as, sitting behind it, PC McGarry (number 452) explains the correct protocol for helping scallies fall downstairs in a single-story nick to Constable Savage, a high flyer who has been transferred from Birmingham to expand out his résumé and help bring policing in Ruralshire into the twentieth century. From his shifty, impatient posture it's obvious that he'd much rather be out on the street monstering chavs. Finally I grow impatient and clear my throat. PC McGarry continues to drone on, obviously enjoying his pulpit far too much to stop, so I pull out my warrant card.

"'Ere, Fred, don't you want to ask this gentleman what he's—" Savage's eyes are drawn to focus on my card wallet and his voice slows to a stop. "What?"

"Bob Howard, Capital Laundry Services. I'd like to speak to Inspector Dudley." I smile assertively. Cops are trained to de-prioritize the unassertive. "If I can have a minute of your attention?"

PC McGarry glances at me, clearly irritated by the interruption. "We don't need any dry-cleaning—"

I focus on him, borrowing the full weight of my ID card's glamor: "Never said you did, mate. *I need to see Inspector Dudley.* As soon as possible, about a matter of some considerable importance. He won't thank you for delaying me."

McGarry doesn't want to yield, but my warrant card isn't going to let him ignore me. "What's it about?" He demands.

"DEFRA want all the vaccination records for the new rides he's commissioning for the mounted unit," I deadpan. "I just missed him at Edgebaston Farm, but the long arm of the livestock law has a way of catching up."

McGarry eyeballs me dubiously, then picks up the phone. "Inspector? There's a Mr. Hobson from DEFRA down here in reception, says he needs to talk to you—something about Edgehill Farm? No sir, I don't. Yes, sir." He puts the phone down. "You. The inspector will be down in a minute." He points at a chair. "Have a seat."

"Don't mind if I do." I ignore the chair and walk over to the noticeboard, to read the public information posters while I wait. (STRANGER DANGER! and REMEMBER TO LOCK YOUR DOORS AND WINDOWS: RURALSHIRE REGULARLY GETS VISITED BY TOWNIE SCUM vie for pride of place with IS YOUR NEIGHBOR EMPLOYING

ILLEGAL IMMIGRANTS? It's like their public relations office moonlights from the BNP.)

I don't have to wait long. I hear footsteps, and as I turn, I hear a familiar voice. "You. What do you want?" Inspector Dudley looks somewhat more intimidating in uniform, and he was plenty intimidating before. He stares down at me coldly from behind the crooked bridge of his nose. Luckily I don't intimidate quite as easily as I used to.

"Perhaps we should talk in your office?" I suggest. "It's about the EMOCUM Units you've requisitioned." I'm still holding my warrant card, and I spot his eyes flickering towards it, then away, as if he's deliberately pretending he hasn't noticed it.

"Come with me," he says. I follow the inspector past the reception area and into the administrative guts of the station: whitewashed partition walls, doors with numbers and frosted glass panels. The cells are presumably downstairs. He heads through a fire door and up a narrow staircase, then into an office with a single desk, a couple of reception chairs, and a window with a nice view of the Victorian railway station frontage. "Who are you, and what are you doing with that old fraud Scullery?" He demands.

"I'm from a department you probably haven't heard of before and mustn't speak about in public." I shove my card right under his nose, where he can't miss it. "The, ah, EMOCUM Units were not authorized by my department. As we have licensing and oversight responsibility for *all* such assets, I want to know where you heard about them, where you got them from, and how you're planning on deploying them." I smile to defuse the sting of my words. "All the paperwork and oversight reports you were making an end-run around have just caught up with you, I'm afraid."

"But the—" He sits down behind the desk, and something in his expression changes. A moment of openness passes, like the shadow of a cloud drifting across a hillside. His expression is closed to me. "What are you doing here? Everything is under control. There's no problem at all."

"I'm afraid I disagree." I keep my warrant card in plain sight. "Tell me: where did you source the EMOCUM Units? And who came up with the proposal in the first place?"

"It seemed like a goodooodood…" His eyes are drawn to the card, even as he stutters: "It was my idea! I'm sure it was. It seemed like such a good idea, so it must have been mine, mustn't it?"

"Really?"

"I thought-ought—" he's fighting the geas on the warrant card as hard as I've ever seen from anyone—"we-e should have a major capability upgrade! Yes, that's it! The Air Support Unit get all the attention these days, them bleeding flyboys! Their choppers can't manage more than four hours' airborne patrol time in 24 hours, and you can't use 'em to make arrests or for crowd control, but they suck the money out of *my* budget. It's us or them! Do you have any idea how much it costs to operate a mounted patrol? To put eight officers on saddles at a match I need twelve mounts because horses aren't like cars, oh no they're not—cars don't suffer from poll evil or grass sickness—and I need at least as many officers as rides. We need civilian auxiliaries because stables don't muck themselves out, on-call vets, and six bales of hay a day. Not to mention the ongoing maintenance bill and depreciation on our motorized horse box and the two trailers, plus the two pickups to tow them."

He begins to foam at the mouth as he winds up to a fine rant about the operational costs of maintaining a mounted unit: "In the last financial year my unit cost nearly six hundred thousand pounds, in order to provide three thousand six hundred mounted officer-shifts of six hours' duration each! The fly-boys cost eight hundred and twenty in return for which we get eleven hundred airborne hours a year and they are weaseling to have my unit decommissioned and our entire budget diverted to running a second Twin Squirrel. I ask you, is *that* a good use of public funds? Or, I ask you this in all sincerity, would it be better spent on equipping our mounted officers with *the best steeds for getting the job done?*"

The inspector slams his open palm down on his desk, making the wilting begonias jump. He glares at me, the whites of his eyes showing. His pupils are dilated and his cheeks are flushed. He gasps for breath before continuing. I watch, somewhere midway between concern and fascination. This is *not* business as usual. What I'm witnessing is symptomatic of an extremely powerful occult compulsion that has been applied to the inspector. His words are powerful: I feel my ward vibrating on its chain, warming up painfully where it lies close to the skin of my chest.

"It is our duty to protect the public and enforce the Law of the Land! Duty, honor, courage in the service of Queen and Country! *The Queen!* I swore an oath to uphold the Law and I will uphold it to the best of my ability! That means enhancing our capabilities wherever possible, striving for maximum efficiency in the delivery of mounted police capabilities! We're barely keeping our heads above water in the face of a deluge of filth coming up from the big cities, darkies and gippos and yids and hippies and, and—*Law and Order!* We must maintain Law and Order! The Queen is coming! *The Queen is coming!* Equipping my division with EMOCUM Units will result in a great increase in our speed, mobility, and availability to enforce the Law of the Land in the coming strugg-ugg-uggle against-against *the forces of darknesssss*—"

His left cheek begins to twitch, and he starts to slur his words. I hastily flip my warrant card upside-down, then pull it back. The pressure from the ward pushing against my sternum subsides as Inspector Dudley slumps sideways, gasping for breath. For a few horrified seconds I'm afraid he's having a stroke: but the twitching subsides and he straightens slowly, leaning against the back of his chair.

"What was I saying?" He asks, looking around hesitantly, as if puzzled to find himself in his own office. "Who are you?"

I take a gamble and hold up my warrant card: "Bob Howard. Who I am is unimportant. You don't need to know. But—" I lean forward—"where did you get the EMOCUM Units from?"

"I, I asked around." He sounds vague and disoriented. "They were just *there* when I needed them." His eyes roll back momentarily: "Sent by the Q-Queen," he adds conversationally, in a tone that makes my skin crawl. He abruptly blinks back to full consciousness: "I don't know where they came from. Why?"

I try again. "Where did the requirements document for the EMOCUM Units come from?"

"I, uh, I've got it somewhere. There." He points a shaky finger at the grubby PC on one side of his desk. "It took ages to write—"

"Would you mind opening the file for me?" I ask. "In Word." I tense up, then haul out my phone as he reaches for the keyboard. It's a flashy new Palm Treo, and I've got some rather special software on it that can scan for certain types of occult hazard (in conjunction with the special-issue box of bluetooth-connected sensors in my jacket pocket). I punch up a utility (icon: *this is your brain on drugs*, superimposed over a red inverted pentacle) and aim my phone's camera at his monitor as he pokes unsteadily at the keyboard.

The inspector is so oblivious to my presence that I might as well not be here—except when he's forced to pay attention to me by my warrant card. This is, in itself, a serious warning sign: he's meant to be one of ours, dammit, and a Laundry warrant card is enchanted with a *geas* that compels subjects to recognize the lawful bearer as a superior officer in their own department. (Except within the Laundry itself, obviously—otherwise we could get into horrifying recursive loops of incrementally ascending seniority: imagine the consequences if this affected Accounting and Payroll!) Anyway, if Jack Dudley's mind is shying away from me, then someone has probably tried to install countermeasures against other adepts' glamors. Which is *really bad news*, because unicorns don't do subtle like that.

So I'm paying more attention to my phone—which is scanning for threat patterns—than to the screen the inspector is squinting at, when the familiar logo of Microsoft Office flashes up for a few seconds, followed in rapid succession by a window onto hell.

MINISTRY OF DEFENCE
SECRET
Procurement Specification: R/NBC/6401

Date of Issue: April 2nd, 1970

Requirement for:

Proposal for Strategic Deterrent (class: alternative, non-nuclear) Type: Anthropic Eschatological Weapons System, Air-Dropped

In view of the increase in popular support for the Campaign for Nuclear Disarmament, it might at some future date be deemed politically expedient for the UK to decommission its strategic nuclear capability in the form of the Resolution-class submarines and their associated Polaris A3 SLBMs. However, the UK's strategic deterrent posture must be maintained at all costs in the face of the Soviet threat.

Chemical weapons are not fit for purpose in this role due to difficulty in ensuring delivery in adequate quantity. Conventional biological weapons (weaponized smallpox, plague, etc.) are not fit for purpose in this role due to the impossibility of immunizing the entire UK population and also of guaranteeing efficacy in the face of an enemy biowar vaccination defense program.

This requirement is for proposals for unconventional macrobiological weapons that are suitable for delivery by manned bomber/stand-off bomb (e.g. Blue Steel), which must undergo post-delivery amplification and inflict strategic-level damage on the enemy, which are not susceptible to pharmaceutical or medical defense, and which are self-limiting (unlikely to give rise to pandemics).

Desirable characteristics:

AEWS-AD must be storable, long-term (temperature/ humidity constraints: see schedule A) without maintenance for up to 5 years.

Must be containerized in suitable form for mounting and delivery via WE.177 bomb casing *or* alternative equivalent structural unit compatible with bomb bay and wing hardpoints on all current operational strike aircraft and the forthcoming Panavia Tornado IDS.

Must be sterile/non-self-replicating *or* must replicate once, giving rise to infertile spawn.

A strike delivering a single AEWS-AD must be capable of depopulating a first-rank capital city (population ablation coefficient: at least 25%) in less than 24 hours.

AEWS-AD should additionally have three or more of the following traits: carnivorous, venomous, mind-controlling, invisible, pyrogenic, flying, basilisk gaze, bullet-resistant, radiation-tolerant for up to 20,000 REM (single pulse) or 1000 rads/hr (fallout), invulnerable to class 6 or lower occult induction algorithms.

State of Requirement

Null and void.

CANCELLED April 3rd, 1970

by Order of Cabinet Office in accordance with recommendation of SOE (X Division) Operational Oversight Audit Committee

Reasons for cancellation order:

The risk of unintentional containment violation or accidental release during the life of such a weapons system is low but nevertheless unacceptably high.

Deployment of AEWS-AD, whether in accordance with legal national command authority or otherwise, would constitute a violation of Section IV.B of the Benthic Treaty. This would deliver a guaranteed *casus belli* to BLUE HADES.

The probability of BLUE HADES retaliation for a violation of S.IV.B leading to the total extinction of the population of the British Isles is 100%, within the limits of error. This applies to the Republic of Ireland, the Isle of Man, the Channel Isles, and Great Britain and Northern Ireland. But this is not the limit of the extent of casualties from such a strike.

The probability of a BLUE HADES strike resulting in the total extinction of the entire human species exceeds 50%.

It is considered that attempting to develop a weapons system in the same category as AEWS-AD is so inherently destabilizing that such activities may be seen as justifying a pre-emptive strike by other human governments. Far from securing the realm against the threat of Soviet nuclear aggression, this project might actually provoke it.

(Addendum: *SOE (X Division) OOAC recommends that it would be in the nation's best interests if all the members of the committee that drafted R/NBC/6401 could be induced to take early retirement; thereafter they should be denied access to sharp instruments.* We are serious about this. *Not since RARDE's BLUE PEACOCK project of 1954 to 1958 has this oversight body been asked to evaluate such an unedifying, if not actually insane, proposal.*)

While I'm glancing down at my smartphone's two-inch screen, Inspector Dudley is helping me with my enquiries by opening up the Microsoft Word file containing the requirements document he remembers drafting for replacing the Sussex constabulary's remaining horses with unicorn spawn—sorry, EMOCUM Units. What could possibly go wrong with *that*?

Well, I find out as the file opens. Because Jack Dudley may remember writing it, but unless he's a skilled battle magus as well as a police inspector, he sure as hell didn't write the Visual BASIC macro that fires up the instant the text appears on screen.

It all gets very messy, very fast.

Because I'm staring at my Treo instead of the PC, I feel it vibrate in my hand as the screen flashes red: THAUM OVERFLOW. I hear a loud whining buzz from the desktop, like a mosquito the size of a Boeing 737, then the unmistakable screech and click of a hard disk shredding its platters: *funny, I didn't know you could do that in software any more*, I just have time to register, as my ward heats up painfully. A second later, Inspector Dudley moans. It's a familiar, extremely unwelcome kind of moan, and it sends shivers up my spine because I hear it late at night when I've been working overtime, on a regular basis. It's the inhuman sound of a soul-sucked husk that hungers for brains, just like the Residual Human Resources on the Night Watch.

This isn't the first time I've seen this happen. You wouldn't believe the scope for mischief that the Beast of Redmond unintentionally builds into its Office software by letting it execute macros that have unlimited access to the hardware. I remember a particular post-prandial PowerPoint presentation where I was one of only two survivors (and the other wasn't entirely human). However, this is the first time I've seen a Word document eat a man's soul.

I straighten up and take two steps backwards. The doorknob grinds against my left buttock: *dammit, why couldn't the door open outwards?* I raise my phone and hastily stroke the D-pad, tracking down the app I need...and the fucking thing crashes on me. *Oh joy.* PalmOS: always there right when you least need it.

The inspector is rising from his seat, clumsily pushing himself away from his desk. His movements are jerky if not tetanic. He moans softly, continuously, and as he turns his head towards me I register the faint greenish glow in his eyes. I grasp the doorknob and freeze, a train-wreck of thoughts piling into each other in my mind's eye.

The CrossRail commuter train leaving Platform One is scared shitless because it's trapped in an office with a genuine no-shit mind-eating zombie, and the law of skin-to-skin contagion means that if the thing touches me I stand to literally lose my mind. This is mitigated slightly by the Sprinter to Crewe on Platform Two, which reminds me that I'm wearing a ward, so I might actually survive, if the zombie doesn't simply double down on my throat or drag me in front of the PC monitor, which is presumably still displaying the same summoning grid that ate Inspector Dudley's mind. The Gatwick Express steaming along the track between Platforms Four and Five at a non-stop ninety miles per hour sounds its air-horn to remind me that if I cut and run I will be leaving the aforementioned zombie unrestrained in a target-rich environment, namely a Ruralshire cop shop where their policy on undead uprisings is to order out for beer and pizza while watching *Shaun of the Dead* in the station house lounge once a month. And the train speeding out of Trumpton with a cargo of cocaine (thank you, Half Man Half Biscuit) is merely there to remind me that I still don't know where the spawn of the unicorn are coming from...

"Raaarrrrh." Inspector Dudley clears his throat and takes an experimental lurch towards me. I dodge sideways behind his desk, pocketing my phone in order to free up a hand, and simultaneously yank the power cord out of the back of his PC. (Rule 1: preserve the evidence, even if the hard disk has self-destructed and the file you want is loaded with a lethally contagious mind-virus.) "Raaargh?" The inspector calls.

I pick up the heavy old tube monitor and heft it in both arms. "Catch," I say, and throw it at the zombie.

I wince at the crunch as twenty kilos of lead-glass CRT impacts the already-broken nose. Dudley staggers and topples backwards: zombies, possessed as they are by a minimally-sentient and rather corporeally challenged Eater, tend not to be fast on their feet. Then the door opens.

"Inspector?" chirps Constable Savage. Then he spots me. I see the ten-watt bulb flicker fitfully to life above his head as he instantly jumps to the wrong conclusion. "Oi! You! Get on the floor! You're nicked!"

He begins to draw his baton as I back away, around the desk, closer to the window. I reach for my warrant card: "You're making a mist—"

"GRAAAAH!" Roars the inspector, rising from the floor, CRT clutched to his chest. *Oh look, he appears to have a nosebleed*, gibbers the shunting engine in Siding Three. *You're in for it now.*

"Inspector?" Asks Constable Savage, "are you all right?"

There's a chime from my pocket, the beautiful sound of a Treo announcing that it has rebooted successfully. "He's a zombie!" I yell. "Don't let him touch you! His touch is death—"

Ignoring me, Savage reaches out towards the inspector: "'Ere, let me look at the *no-o-o*—"

Great. Now I'm facing two of them.

If my boss Angleton was here this wouldn't be a problem: one glance from him is sufficient to quell zombie brain-eater and union convenor alike. But I'm not some kind of superpowered necromancer, I'm just a jobbing sysadmin and applied computational demonologist. About the only card I'm holding is—

Well, it's worth a try.

I raise my warrant card and rehearse my rusty Old Enochian: "Guys! I am your lawful source of authority! Obey me! Obey me!" (Or words to that effect.) It's a horrible language, sounds like gargling TCP around razor blades. But it gets their attention. Two heads turn to face me. Their eyes glow even in daylight, the luminous worms of light twirling inside them. "Proceed to the stable block! Enter the first empty stall! Await your queen! Await your queen! Your queen is coming and she must find you there!" Then in English I add, "Law and Order! Law and Order!"

The last bit comes out like "lawn order," but repeating the catchphrase deeply embedded in what's left of the inspector's brain by the *geas* that had him in its grip seems to do the trick.

"Graah?" He says, with a curious rising interrogative note. Then he turns to face the door. "Ssss…" Clumsy fingers scrabble with the smooth surface of the old doorknob. The door inches open. I hope to hell nobody else is about to stumble into them on their way to the field-expedient cells. I really don't want this spreading any further. The fear-sweat in the small of my back is cold and slimy, and I feel faint and nauseous.

Constable Savage lost interest in his baton the moment he touched the inspector: I pick it up and follow them as they lurch and stumble down the staircase and out past the vacant front desk. As we pass the gents' toilet I hear a musical tinkling: *Phew.* Presumably that's McGarry on his break, in which case there may be survivors. With the odd moan, hiss, and growl, the two zombies cross the courtyard, lurching off the side of a parked riot van, and head towards an empty horse stall. I nip in front of them to unbolt the gate and open it wide. There's nothing inside but a scattering of hay, and the shamblers keep on going until they bounce off the crumbling brick wall at the back—by which time I have the gate shut and bolted behind them.

I pull out my Treo and speed-dial the Duty Officer's desk back at the New Annexe. "Bob Howard speaking," I say, "I'm in the Central Police Station in East Grinstead and I'm declaring a Code Amber, repeat, Code Amber. We have an outbreak, outbreak, outbreak. Code words are EQUESTRIAN RED SIRLOIN. I have two Romeo Hotel Romeo, outbreak contained, and a hot box on the second floor. I need plumbers, stat."

Then I head back up the stairs to the ex-inspector's office to secure the PC with the lethally corrupt file system, and await the arrival of the Seventh Cavalry, all the while sweating bullets.

Because I may have taken two pawns, but the queen is still lurking in the darkness at the edge of the chess-board...

MINISTRY OF DEFENCE
SECRET
Procurement Specification: N/SBS/007

Date of Issue: September 31st, 2002

Requirement for:

Proposal for system to support Special Boat Service underwater operations in the Arabian Gulf during Operation Telic.

S Squadron SBS, in accordance with orders from the Director Special Forces, is tasked with securing [REDACTED] on the coastline of Umm Quasr and Hajjam Island, and suppressing the operational capability of the Sixth Republican Guard Fast Motor Boat and Martyrdom

Brigade to sortie through the Shatt Al-Basra and the Khawr az-Zubayr Waterway to threaten Coalition naval forces in Kuwaiti waters.

This requirement is for proposals for unconventional macrobiological weapons that operate analogously to the Ceffyl Dŵr, Capaill Uisce and Kelpie of mythology. These organisms are amphibious but preferentially aquatic, carnivorous, aggressive, intelligent, and reputed to drag sailors under water and drown them. It is believed that with suitable operant conditioning and control by S Squadron troopers such organisms can provide a useful stand-off capability to augment the capabilities of underwater special forces operating in a dangerous high-intensity littoral combat environment...

State of Requirement

Null and void.

CANCELLED October 13th, 2002

by Order of Cabinet Office in accordance with recommendation of SOE (X Division) Operational Oversight Audit Committee

Reasons for cancellation order:

1. Baby-eating aquatic faerie equines *do not exist.*
2. Even if they *did* exist, it is worth noting that Arab folklore and mythology does not emphasize fear of death by drowning; consequently the psywar potential of this proposal is approximately zero.
3. Operational requirement can be met through already-existing conventional means.

(Addendum: *Going forward, SOE (X Division) OOAC recommends a blanket ban on all procurement specifications that involve supernatural equine entities (SEEs). For reference, see EQUESTRIAN RED SIRLOIN. This keeps coming up like a bad penny at least once every couple of decades, and it's got to stop.*)

Forty minutes pass. I while away the time by making panicky phone calls to our INFOSEC desk—how the hell did that macro virus get into the file on the inspector's PC? I love the smell of an enquiry in the morning—while I wait in Inspector Dudley's office, sweating bullets. Finally I hear the heart-warming song of two-tone sirens coming down the high street. It's not the warbling war-cry of police blues and twos, but the regular rise and fall of a fire engine—which means my prayers have been answered, and the Plumbers are coming, in the shape of an OCULUS truck.

From the outside it looks like a bright red Fire Service Major Incident Command vehicle, but it's not crewed by Pugh, Pugh, Barney McGrew, Cuthbert, Dibble, and Grub—this one's occupants are the away team of 21 Territorial SAS, and they're more likely to start fires than extinguish them. I watch as it drives nose-first into the police station car park and stops. Doors open and half a dozen wiry-looking guys dressed head to foot in black leap out. They're armed to the teeth. One of them looks up at me and I wave. While I've been waiting I filled in the Duty Officer back at HQ with as much as I knew. Now Sergeant Howe and his men fan out and move through the nearly-empty police station. Two of them dash for the stall where I stashed the shamblers, carrying a field exorcism kit in a duffle bag. The others...I hear doors banging and much shouting as they go through the station like a tide of Ex-Lax.

I move to the desk and sit down behind it facing the door, making sure to keep my hands in view, and hold up my warrant card. I sit like this for approximately thirty seconds before it crashes open and I find myself staring up the business end of an MP5K. "Oops, sorry sir. Be right back." The MP5K and its owner disappear as I try to get my heart rate back down to normal.

Finally, after another minute, the door opens again—this time more sedately. "Hello, Bob!" It's Alan Barnes, chipper and skinny, with slightly hyperthyroidal eyes. He bounces into the room, head swiveling. "Nice pair of shamblers you've penned up down there. What do I need to know?"

Alan is a captain in that corner of the Army that we work with when this sort of situation comes up: namely one particular squadron of the Territorial SAS, a peculiar special forces unit composed of reservist veterans who have seen more and stranger things than most of their colleagues would credit with existing. His crew of merry pranksters are securing the premises as we speak. "There's a file on this computer," I say, patting the box on the desk. "You heard about the business in Darmstadt with the infected PowerPoint presentation?" He nods. "Well, there's a Word document with an infected startup macro on this thing's hard disk. Which it attempted to scribble on when the inspector—in the stables right now—tried to open it for me." He nods again, looking thoughtful. "This needs Forensics to go over it. We're looking for a requirements document which seems to have come out of nowhere, and which persuaded Inspector Dudley that it was all his own idea to replace the horses in his mounted unit with, ah, EMOCUM Units. Otherwise known as the subjects of EQUESTRIAN RED SIRLOIN."

Alan has a notepad. "How do you spell that?" He murmurs politely.

I fill him in as fast as possible. "DEFRA spotted it, there's an emergent cuckoo's nest down on Edgebaston Farm but the farm owner doesn't seem to be infected—" *yet* "—so I suggest once we've secured the station we rendezvous with Greg Scullery and proceed to the farm to conduct a full suppression. What remains after that is to—" my shoulders slump—"work out where the hell the brood-Queen's spawning-nest is, and take *her* out." I swallow, then continue: "Which is bound to be harder than it was in Lovecraft's day, if only because the thing has concealed its tracks well, and appears to be pulling the puppet strings of local Renfields like the Inspector. If it figures out we're coming it may be able to organize a defense. In the worst case scenario, East Grinstead is going up in flames. And that's before we get to the thorny question of where that demon-haunted requirements document came from."

Alan sits down on the wobbly swivel chair with no armrests. "I'm not familiar with, ah, EQUESTRIAN RED SIRLOIN," he admits. "I'll need to get clearance and then—"

We don't have time. On the other hand, ERS is barely classified at all. I pull out my briefing papers: "On my cognizance, and in view of the severity of the situation, with a class two Eater outbreak in train, I take full responsibility for disclosing EQUESTRIAN RED SIRLOIN. Or, at least, what *I* know about it," I add hastily. (Because if it *is* an inside job, (a.) I don't know enough to blow its cover, and (b.) it's just very publicly shat the bed, and whoever is running it is probably in for the high jump whatever I do. In other words, my and Alan's attempts at mopping up are unlikely to make the mess any worse.)

Alan raises an eyebrow. "Are you sure?"

I shrug. "It's classified MILDLY EMBARRASSING NO TABLOIDS. I'm sure they'll offer me a cigarette and a blindfold at the firing squad."

Alan nods and takes the papers. "Right," he drawls. What I'm doing is technically unauthorized, but my Oath of Office lets me get away with it without even a warning tingle. I'm pretty sure Iris will sign off on it when I file my report. And if not, I can't see the Auditors yelling at me for briefing my field support team. Then his eyes focus on the first page, and the list of decreasing classification levels, and the index of documents attached, and his eyebrows climb so high they nearly merge with his hairline. *"Unicorns?* Bob, what have you gotten us into *this* time?"

"I wish I knew, Alan. But they're not sparkly…"

RING-RING. "YES, WHO is that?"

"Greg? It's Bob here. Where are you?"

"I'm back at the office, sorting out some paperwork. Has something come up?"

"You could say that. Listen, can you meet me at the old police station? As soon as possible; it's urgent. There are some gentlemen I'd like to introduce you to. We want your input on operation planning."

"I—yes, I daresay I could do that, young feller. Is five o'clock too late?"

I glance at Alan. He nods, minutely controlled. "Five o'clock but no later," I say. We exchange pleasantries: "See you. Bye." I glance at my phone: it's ten past four. Back at Alan: "In my opinion, we're not ready to go public," I explain. "No point frightening the bystanders."

"Hmm." Alan gives in to toe-tapping and thumb-twiddling, impatient tics that seem to vanish whenever an actual operation starts. "Let's go over the map again, shall we?"

We've got an Ordnance Survey 1:12,500 spread out across the table in the antique briefing room. A couple of constables have shown up for shift change, and we've taken pains to explain the situation to them in words of one syllable: a chief inspector from a mega-city like Hove or Brighton is on her way in to take control of the policing side of the operation, but I gather she's caught up in traffic, so for now we're relying on

Sergeant Colon to keep everything looking vaguely like business as usual. Alan's driver finally un-wedged the OCULUS truck from the cobblestoned yard, and it's parked outside. The contingency story for the reporter from the *Bexhill Babble* is that we're conducting a joint major incident containment exercise simulating an outbreak of anthrax on a local farm. Which is close enough to the truth to make what we're really doing look plausibly routine if not actually boring, so that when we get the officers of the law to cordon off Edgebaston Farm nobody will so much as blink.

The map is accurate enough to let Alan's merry headbangers lay down a barrage of covering fire if that's what it takes. I point out the various elements of the farm. "The barn: there are two or more EMOCUM Units stationed there. Carnivorous, fast, hopefully hobbled. The woodshed: has damp rot in the roof beams. Currently full of lumber, they're planning on putting the cows in it when they get round to emptying it. South field: two horses, four cows (one of them with a wooden leg). Basically harmless. The EMOCUM Units are distinctive—the eyes are too close together and glow blue, and their fur is white—"

"Don't you mean they're cremelo? Or at least perlino?" Alan raises an eyebrow at me.

"Whatever." I shrug. "They look like horses, walk like horses, have breath like a leopard. Oh, there'll also be saddles with roll cages stashed in the barn—"

"Roll cages?" His eyebrows are really getting a workout today.

"With wire mesh reinforcement, yes, to stop the nice horsies eating their riders. Seriously, if any of your men see a horse-shaped object that can't *instantly* be confirmed safe, they should shoot to kill. We're dealing with the Hannibal Lecters of the riding world here."

"Moving swiftly on—" Alan points at the farm house itself. "What can you tell me about this structure?"

"Oh, *that*. Farmhouse, repeatedly built, razed, re-built, extended, and re-razed ever since the twelfth century. AD, not BC, though you might be hard put to tell. Main entrance opens into a porch with boot racks, closet to the left, huge farm kitchen to the right, passage leading into house at the back, and no, before you ask, I didn't get a good look inside. Why do you—"

"People," Alan interrupts conversationally. "Who am I dealing with here?"

"Apart from Georgina Edgebaston herself, who is apparently as well-connected as a System X exchange, I have no idea. Farm hand called Adam, daughter called Octavia who's at boarding school, I gather. We'll really need to pick Greg's brain. And the—no, police records'll be no use." I shrug. (The Edgebastons are the sort of people the police work for, not against. And you don't keep files on your boss if you know what's good for you.) "If we can get anything useful out of Inspector Dudley—"

Alan shakes his head. "Sandy confirms the exorcism worked, but both victims are in bad shape. The ambulance should be arriving at St. Hilda's any time now." He glances at his wristwatch. "Okay, so it's a centuries-old farmhouse. Which means any floor plan on file with the County planning office will be years or decades out of date, if they even bothered filing one in the first place."

"Why are you focusing on the farmhouse?" I ask, feigning casual interest.

He flashes me a smile. "Because if there's one thing all the unicorn legends are clear about, it's the little girl! The, ah, broodqueen's primary host. Do you know what boarding school Mrs. Edgebaston's daughter attends?"

I suddenly realize where he's going with this line of enquiry. "Let's find out, and confirm that she's really there." My phone's really getting a workout. I call the Duty Officer back at head office and pass the buck. (Let someone else fight their way through social services and school phone switchboards this afternoon.) "And let's hope there's no brood-queen to mop up. Ahem. So where are we going with this?"

"Here." Alan points at the various gates leading into the fields around Edgebaston farm. "First: I'm going to station police officers on all the B-roads leading past the fields. Cover Story Alpha applies and will justify the operation. The south field gate will also have two of my people, armed, in case of attempted equine excursions. I take your point about friend/foe discrimination. Secondly: OCULUS units one and two, accompanied by your tame veterinary inspector, will move in on the farmyard. Brick two will secure the exterior of the barn, brick three will take the other outbuildings, while the rest of us serve a search warrant on the farmhouse itself and conduct a room-to-room inspection." The SAS doesn't deal in fire teams and squads and platoons, it divvies up into bricks (more formally patrols) and troops and squadrons.

"Wait, you're pulling in a second OCULUS?"

Alan's cheek twitches. "After reading that file, I'd be happier to simply call in an air strike."

The office door opens and a familiar face appears: "Scary" Spice, whom I have worked with before, and who has a penchant for blowing stuff up. "Sir? The XM-1060s have arrived. Sergeant Howe has detailed Norton and Simms to load and fuse them, he wanted you to know they'll be safed but ready when you need them." He spots me. "Hi, Bob!" Then he ducks out again.

"What are they?" I ask.

Alan twitches again: "Thermobaric grenade launchers. Just in case."

Now *my* cheek twitches. It's a sympathy thing, triggered by my involuntary ringpiece clenching. "Is that really necessary?"

"I hope not, Bob. I hope not…"

WHICH IS WHY, at a whisker after six o'clock in the evening, I come to be sitting in the front passenger seat of Mr. Scullery's Land Rover, which is bumping and jouncing across a pasture that clings precariously to the side of Mockuncle Hill. I am holding Greg's rifle for him because he is gesticulating wildly with both hands while trying to steer with his beard. The steering wheel, unaccustomed to such treatment, squeals and tries to escape every time we bump across a post hole. "Never heard anything like it!" He expostulates wildly: "Young Barnes is overreacting *wildly*."

"In case you hadn't noticed, he's running this show."

"In *my* day he was a wet-behind-the-ears cornet, young feller—"

I roll my eyes as the beard describes Alan's prehistoric sins, from back when dinosaurs roamed the earth and Greg was in the service. "Listen," I interrupt between tooth-rattling jolts, "let's just stick to business, okay?" I scan the field for alien life forms such as cows, three-legged or otherwise, and the retired police horses we've been told to expect here.

The sun is setting, behind the bulk of the hill. There's still light in the sky, but the shadows have become indistinct and hazy, and a golden glow washes out all contrast as it slowly dims towards full dark. The lights will be flickering to life on the streets in town. This is a really stupid time of day for us to be doing this, but Alan wants to get it underway ASAP, and will be turning up at the farmhouse door in another five minutes.

Behind us, a jam sandwich has parked up across the lane, light
bar flickering as the constables tape off the entrance to the field.
Our job is to round up the local legal livestock and neutralize
them safely so that Alan's merry men don't mistake them for
equoids. Hence the tranquilizer gun and the vet.

(I also half-suspect that Alan has sent Greg and me on this
wild horse chase to keep us out of his hair during the somewhat
more fraught process of storming a farmhouse without killing
the human occupants.)

I'm just checking the near-side wing mirror when my Treo
rings. I glance at it: it's the Duty Officer back at HQ. My stomach flip-flops. "Howard here," I say.

"We have the information you requested about Octavia
Edgebaston, sir. Sorry it's taken so long; we had to contact
Social Services in East Grinstead out-of-hours to get the contact
details for her school, then get the headmistress out of her din-
ner. Yes, we've confirmed that Octavia Edgebaston is boarding
as St. Ninian's School this week and is currently at prep in room
207—" I breathe a sigh of relief—"but her younger sister—"

"What?" I yelp involuntarily. "Greg! You didn't tell me
Georgina had another daughter!"

"—Is truant, she didn't show up for register this afternoon
and they're extremely worried—"

"What other daughter?" The beard sounds puzzled, almost
dreamy. "There's no other—"

"—Lucinda Edgebaston, class 2E at St. Ninian's, aged
twelve. She hasn't signed out of the school, and they're re-run-
ning the CCTV over the gate now just to check, but she missed
all her afternoon classes—"

"How far away is St. Ninian's from Edgebaston Farm?" I ask.

"Ten or eleven miles," says the DO. "To continue: they've
notified the police in Hove and they're keeping an eye out for

her. One-forty centimeters, long chestnut hair, about fifty kilos, probably wearing St. Ninian's school uniform. She won't have gotten far—"

My heart is pounding and the skin on the back of my neck is crawling. I have a very bad feeling about this. "Please hold," I tell my phone. "Greg: stop. *Stop.*" I thump the middle of the dash. Greg slams on the anchors so suddenly I nearly go through the split windscreen. As it is, the barrel of the rifle bashes my forehead. I'm doubly glad I made sure it was unloaded and safe when he gave it to me to hold. (No, really; there's a luminous pipecleaner going in through the barrel and out of the open breech, because self-inflicted head shots are *so* not one of my favorite things. Actually, I'm not sure how to load it in the first place—it can fire tranquilizer darts as well as bullets—but it's the thought that counts.)

The Landy squeals and slithers to a muddy standstill in the middle of the south field. "What is it, young feller?" Greg asks me.

"Greg, does Georgina have a husband?" I ask. It's an odd question, and as it slides around the back of my skull like a ping-pong ball I feel my ward warm against my collar-bone.

The beard looks puzzled. "I don't rightly—" he pauses— "no, no, that's not *right.*" Another pause. "That would be Jerry, Gerald, I forget his name. Haven't seen him in ages; I suppose they divorced. And then there's Octavia and the other and young Ada."

"Ada? How old is Ada, Greg? Concentrate!"

"Ada's just a toddler, Bob. I think she's four—" The beard scrunches up in violent concentration—"*What!*"

The explosion is so sudden I nearly jump out of my seat. "What?" I echo.

"How could I *forget* them! Georgina is married to Harry and they have three daughters, Octavia and Lucinda and Ada!

Named after her great grand-nan," he adds conversationally. "But, but—"

I'm on the phone to the DO. "Update: I'm seeing signs of a *geas* here. Localized amnesia, level four or higher. Locals have no or restricted memory of adult Harry Edgebaston and minor Ada Edgebaston. There may be other drop-outs." I glance in the wing mirror again: "Lucinda is out of the picture, but—*fuck me,* Greg, *drive!*"

OBJECTS IN MIRROR ARE CLOSER THAN THEY SEEM, and the pallid ghost of Death's own horse is cantering behind us with sapphire-glowing eyes that pulse hypnotically in the twilight. On its back there sits a saddle with roll bars and steel mesh grilles, the rider a small but indistinct figure standing in the stirrups within. The Landy's rear lights flicker red highlights off the point of the lowered lance that's coming towards us as the horse-thing screams a heart-stopping wail of despair and rage.

I drop the phone in my front pocket as Greg floors the throttle and the Landy roars in response, belching a column of smoke that would do justice to a First World War dreadnought. We rock and roll uphill, and the point of the lance rips through the canvas cover over the load bed, then tears away into the night with a snort and huff of equoid heavy breathing.

For an instant, the dash of the Land Rover glows blue-green with a ghastly imitation of St. Elmo's Fire. My skin crawls and the ward heats up painfully. Greg grunts with pain and the steering wheel spins. For a moment the Landy teeters on two wheels, nearly toppling, but then he grabs the wheel with both hands and brings us back down on all fours with a crash.

I fumble with the rifle, yanking the safety cord through the barrel and barking my fingers painfully on the breech. "Ammo, Greg," I gasp.

"In the center cubby, young feller, between the seats. Don't bother with darts." I yank the lid of the compartment between our seats open and rummage around until I feel the oily-smooth metallic weight of an unboxed stripper clip—what kind of bloody idiot keeps loose rifle rounds rolling around his car?—and I somehow manage to reverse the gun over my right shoulder and get the open breech into a position where I can start feeding rounds in. They're the real thing, I hope, but unfortunately there are only five of them. And I can just glimpse a grey-white blur in the twilight at the other end of the field, getting itself turned round to take another run at us—this time a full-tilt charge.

You might think that a mounted cavalry horse charging with lance is a wee bit dated, and less than a match for a bolt-action rifle and a Land Rover. However, you would be very wrong. The thing at the far end weighs over a ton, and it's about to take a run at us at over fifty kilometers per hour. The field is small enough that it's less than a minute away, and when it hits all that momentum is going to be focused behind a tempered steel point. That's about as much energy as a shell from a Second World War tank gun carries: more than enough force to shatter the engine block of an unarmored Landy, and once we're immobilized it can dance around until we're out of bullets, then bite and trample us to death at its leisure.

I close the breech and work the bolt to chamber a round. "Park up and drop the windows. Gun's loaded."

"Easy, young feller." We judder to a halt again. Greg yanks the hand brake, then slides a bolt and the entire windshield assembly flops forwards across the bonnet. "Give me that."

I hand the rifle over. He takes it in both arms and leans forward, barrel pointing across the spare tire. The spectre in front of us turns to face us. The eyes flare, alternating hypnotically. I feel a wave of malevolent intent spill across us. Hocks contract and unwind like spring steel as the equoid launches itself towards us. The spearhead glitters in our headlights, seemingly aimed right in my face. "Think you can hit the rider?" I ask anxiously.

"Piece of piss—" Greg freezes. "Oh no," he breathes.

It takes me another second or two to register what he's seen—his eyesight is better than mine—and I do a double-take because the rider, hunched beneath that odd steel canopy, lance cradled under one elbow like a knight of old…the rider is *too small*. Dwarfed by her mount, in fact. Greg is paralyzed because he's just realized he's drawing a bead on Lucinda Edgebaston, age twelve and a half, who should be in the school dormitory doing her prep rather than galloping across a muddy field on top of a carnivorous horror *that is using her as a human shield—*

A heartbeat passes.

"Give me that." I grab the gun barrel. Greg lets it go without resistance, and that in itself is terribly *wrong*. I shoulder the thing, unaccustomed to its weight and heft. I've done a basic long-arms familiarization course out at the Village, but for the actual range time we used SA80s. It's only by sheer chance that I once asked Harry the Horse to show me how to load one of these antiques. The equoid is expanding in front of me like an oncoming train wreck. I don't have time to check the sights.

I let my breath out slowly and squeeze the trigger, hoping I'll hit something. There's a crash and a bang, and a fully laden freight train slams into my right shoulder. Through the ringing in my ears I hear a wavering inhuman scream, too long-drawn-out for human lungs. Then *another* freight train slams into the side of the Land Rover, and there's a screaming of torn and twisted metal as the thrashing equoid crashes down on us and the Landy topples sideways onto the hillside.

What happens next is a confusing mess. I nearly lose the rifle. I find myself lying on the passenger door, still strapped in, with Greg lying across me. There's blood, blood everywhere, and animal screaming from outside the Land Rover's cabin. "Greg, *move*," I say, and elbow him. More blood: he head-butts my shoulder, and I have a horrible feeling that a human neck shouldn't, can't, bend that way. He is, at the very least, unconscious, and possibly in spinal injury territory. *Shit*. More hoarse screaming. A clanging double-thud that sends a shock through the chassis of the vehicle. I find the seat belt button and try to worm my way forward, through the gap between the open windshield and the roofline, bashing myself in the face yet again with a rifle barrel.

Getting out of a toppled all-terrain vehicle in the dark while a pain-crazed monster bucks and runs around you, occasionally lashing out with its hooves at the felled Land Rover that hurt it, is easier said than done—especially when you're covered in someone else's blood, in need of a change of underwear, and trying to keep control of an unfamiliar weapon. It's so much easier said than done, in fact, that I don't succeed. Or rather, I get my head and shoulders out, along with the rifle, whose bolt I am frantically working when My Little Pony finally notices I'm still alive. It gives a larynx-shattering howl of pure rage, bares a mouthful of spikes that would give a megalodon pause, and closes in for the coup de grace.

I mentioned the rifle, didn't I? And I mentioned that EMOCUM Units aren't the sharpest knife in the toolbox, too? Well, what happens next is about what you'd expect: it's messy, and extremely loud, and I nearly shoot my right ear off as Buttercup bends toward me and opens wide in an attempt to bite my skull in half. Then I have to duck backwards sharpish to avoid being crushed by a ton of falling burger meat.

(Moral of story: if you are a flesh-eating monster, do *not* let the chattering monkey insert a bang-stick in your mouth while you're trying to snack down on its brains. Seriously, no good will come of this.)

MORE CONFUSED IMPRESSIONS:

I'm out of the Landy, standing in the field, frantically looking around. (Two rounds left in the magazine and one up the spout.)

The EMOCUM has collapsed in front of the toppled Land Rover. Brains and other matter show through the back of its shattered skull. I dodge fangs like daggers, and inhale a fecal smell so rich and intense I have to pause to control my stomach. I glance in the roll cage. There is moaning, audible through the ringing in my ears, and I feel dizzy. I look closer. *Movement.* "Lucinda?" I call. "Lucy?"

She looks up at me, one arm bent back unnaturally, still gripping the shaft of the shattered lance: I can see bone. The expression on her face is no more human than her mount's: *"Hssss…"*

"Be right back," I say hastily, stepping away. I fumble for my phone, then speed-dial the last number—the Duty Officer. "Howard here." I briskly explain the situation. "Need medical support with exorcism kit, south field—minor with broken arm and possible demonic possession. Scratch that: probable. Oh, and it'll take the jaws of life to get her out of the saddle." I look around. "One probable adult fatality, cervical fracture, lots of blood." As I feared, when Lucy hit the Landy with her pig-sticker, the impact had had the force of a light artillery shell. "One dead sterile adult Echo Romeo Sierra, one unaccounted for. I'm proceeding afoot and armed."

I look around in the dusk. I see an indistinct hump in the field about thirty meters uphill. A buzz of flies surrounds it, but it's no cow pat; it's the whole damn animal, disemboweled and half-eaten. I bite back a hysterical giggle. This operation has officially fallen apart.

See, the whole idea was to discreetly secure the barn and then search the premises, on the assumption that the EMOCUM Units would be at home. But it now looks as if there's a subtle and nasty amnesia glamor covering parts of the farm, nudging everybody to forget the existence of certain people who have softly and silently been stolen away, presumably because they have seen the boojum.

And now that I think about it, there weren't anything like enough officers hanging around the police station, were there? Not for a mounted unit that needs eighteen riders and a bunch of civilian auxiliaries, never mind the everyday foot and car patrols. There weren't enough folks around the farm, either, and come to think of it Greg's veterinary practice looked half-empty...

My skin crawls. Somewhere out in the gathering twilight an EMOCUM Unit is stalking human prey. And somewhere else—if only I could work out where!—the Queen is brooding.

I'M HALFWAY UP the south field, working my way towards the farm itself, when the sky above me flashes orange, reflecting a dazzling glare from ground level. A second later there's a hollow *whump* like a gas range igniting, and a hot blast of wind across my face. I go to my knees in a controlled fall, land on a cow pat, skid, swear, and faceplant. The explosion rolls up into an ascending fireball that lights up the grass in front of my nose before it dissipates.

I realize what's happening: Alan's men have made hard contact. There's a rattle of small-arms fire, then another of those gas flares followed by a gut-liquefying explosion. They must be the XM-1060's Scary was talking about, I figure. I stay down, but pull my phone up and speak: "Bob here. I'm still in the south field, and the balloon's gone up about three hundred meters north of my current location. Can you let OCULUS Control know I'm out here?" I do not want to be a blue-on-blue casualty. I'm shivering as I speak, and feeling shaky and cold. I work my jaws and spit, trying to get the metallic taste of blood out of my mouth. I'm pretty sure it's Greg's blood. I feel awful about getting him into this, and about leaving him in the Landy.

"Patching you through right away," says the DO, and there's a click.

"Bob? Sitrep!" It's Alan, sounding sharp as a button.

"I'm lying low in the south field about three hundred meters short of the yard. Greg's down, the Landy is down, we nailed one target, there is an injured little girl in the wreckage." I lick my lips, then spit: "Suspect EMOCUM Two is on the loose with a rider, either adult male or juvenile female. There's a stealth glamor on the entire farm; you may not spot the Queen until you step on her." A horrible thought hits me. "The woodshed."

I put it together all at once. No sniggering now: Georgina was planning to clear the woodshed, but *there's damp rot in the roof beams*. And it hasn't been cleared. And the four-year-old is forgotten. And there's "—Something narsty in the woodshed," I hear myself saying aloud into the phone. "Wait for me before you go in!" I add hastily. *Ada. Named for her great-great.* Why should that resonate so—"Alan. Brick three. You sent them to search the outbuildings. Have you heard from them recently?"

"Yes, Bob," he sounds almost bored. "They report all's clear."

"There's a glamor!" I realize I'm shouting. *"Are they in the woodshed?"*

"I'll just...shit."

"I'm on my way," I hear myself saying. "Let your people know I'm coming from the south field on foot." It takes all my willpower to force myself to push upright onto my knees, then to raise one leg, and then the other until I'm standing. I am deathly afraid of what I'm going to find in the farmyard. One foot goes in front of the other. Clump, clump, *squish*, clump. The small-arms fire has stopped, but something ahead is on fire and the flames are playing hell with my night vision. A smell of woodsmoke drifts on the evening breeze, making my nose itch but partly masking the uncanny stink of the field.

I stumble towards the skeletal outline of a gate. It takes me a while to cover the distance because I keep stopping to peer around in the murk, rifle raised. If EMOCUM Unit 2 was in the field with me I expect I'd know about it by now, but you can never be sure. How do feral unicorns stalk their prey, anyway? Do they run in packs, like wolves, or are they ambush hunters?

Beside the gate I stumble across the disemboweled corpse of another cow; Graceless, I think, going by the prosthetic leg. It's upsetting. (You can tell I'm English by the way pointless cruelty to animals dismays me.) The gate itself is hanging open, the chain and padlock neatly fastened around its post. EMOCUM Units don't have hands, so that tears it—we're definitely dealing with ensorcelled human servitors here. And that implies a controlling intelligence, which in turn implies—

The upper story of the west wing of the farmhouse is on fire. The thatching on the roof is smoldering, and the bright light of active combustion is rippling out behind a row of windows. I see the silhouettes of men crouching in the shadows around the barn. A fire engine hulks in the entrance to the yard, around the side of the house. I stand up. My phone rings. "Yes?"

"Get down, idiot." Alan is tense. I drop to my haunches, keeping the rifle barrel vertical. "It's the shed."

"Yeah." *There's something narsty in the woodshed.* "Brick three?"

"Not responding, presumed down." His voice is flat. "I'm behind the barn. Get yourself over here but stay low."

I scurry over to the barn, where I find Alan and Sergeant Howe and a couple of troopers. They're all in body armor and face paint, armed to the incisors with big scary guns. And they look very, *very*, pissed-off.

"There's probably a little girl in there, Alan. Four years old, and all alone in the nest of, of a spawning unicorn Queen." I'm light-headed and feeling careless, otherwise I wouldn't dare speak like that under the circumstances.

"Yes. Also Lance Davies and Troopers Chen, Irving, and Duckworth," he adds. "Do you have anything useful to contribute?"

"Lovecraft's monster implied that a spawning Queen becomes part of a group mind or a swarm intelligence, or somehow becomes conscious, shortly before its offspring eat it. We're now seeing signs of ritual magic—possession, concealment glamor. Let's put that down to the sidereal age—" CASE NIGHTMARE GREEN, when the stars are coming right and all things esoteric become dangerously accessible—"and speculate that the thing H. P. Lovecraft called Shub-Niggurath is using the thing in that woodshed as a vector." I swallow. "And it's in this farm. What I'm wondering is, what's it going to do now? We've got it encircled, but unlike the sterile females, it's not stupid. And it knows it's going to die. Its whole raison d'etre is to maximize the number of its spawn who mate and survive…"

I trail off.

A little girl, a toddler really, who is under the power of the thing in the woodshed. Her elder sister should be at St. Ninian's girl's boarding school, but has instead gone AWOL and turned up on the family farm, riding an EMOCUM, in the middle of term-time, just as we began to investigate. I shudder. "Someone needs to go over—" I stop. "Shit!"

"Bob! Explain."

"Lucinda is down on EMOCUM One in the South Field. Octavia *was* in prep an hour ago, but EMOCUM Two is missing. You know about schools and cross-infection? How if a kid goes to school with an infection, all their classmates and then everyone else catches it? If you wanted to massively amplify a unicorn infestation, about the best way to go about it would be to dump a ton of fertilized unicorn spawn on the doorstep of a girls' boarding school. Especially with the TV series and movies and magazine spin-offs doing the rounds right now." I spit again. "But the teachers and staff wouldn't let a girl bring a live pet into a boarding school. She'd have to smuggle them in some time after the start of term, hide them in the saddle bags, or send for a magic steed and go collect them in person."

Sergeant Howe stares at me like I've grown a second head, but Alan just nods. "You should double-check on that," he says. "Be rather awkward if we had to firebomb a boarding school." He taps his throat mike: "Alpha to all, flash, incoming hostile on horseback. Shoot the horse on contact, assume rider possessed. Over."

I'm on my phone to the DO again. "Howard here. Please can you double-check that Octavia Edgebaston is still doing her prep in her dorm? This is an emergency. If she's missing we need to know immediately. Also: any reports of white horses with glowing blue eyes riding cross-country—"

"Will do! Anything else I can help you with?"

I sigh. "That's all for now." I hang up, then look at Alan. "Why haven't you burned the nest already?"

"Well, now." Alan looks at Howe. "Sergeant, if you'd care to explain the little problem to Mr. Howard?"

Howe sucks his teeth and looks pained. "It's like this, Bob me old mate: it's a woodshed. Wood: made of cellulose, right? Burns if you ignite it?" I nod like a bobble-head. "Well, they also stored other things in there. Inadvisable things. This is a farm, and for fertilizer they use—"

"Oh no," I say, as he continues—

"Ammonium nitrate. About a ton of it. Harry Edgebaston moved it into the woodshed a month ago, last thing anyone remembers seeing him do." Howe bares his teeth. "It'll make a bit of a mess if it brews up."

Alan grins humorlessly. "Your theory that the thing in the woodshed is growing more intelligent and more powerful just got a boost, Bob. What do you propose to do about it?"

I'm about to swither and prevaricate for a bit when my phone rings again. It's the DO. I listen to what he has to say, then thank him and look at Alan. "A riderless stray horse jumped the gates at St. Ninian's about fifteen minutes ago. When it left, it had a bareback rider. So I reckon, let's see, ten miles…you've got maybe five to ten minutes to get ready for Octavia and EMOCUM Unit Two. They'll be trying to get to the barn." I bare my teeth. "I want a sample retrieval kit, and some extras. Then I'm going to go and talk to the monster while you guys neutralize Octavia and her ride. If I stop transmitting, pull back to a safe distance and use the woodshed for target practice. Any questions?"

FIVE MINUTES LATER, I'm ready. At Alan's sign, two of his troopers pull the woodshed door open in front of me. I step forward, into the stygian darkness within.

This is a pretty dumb thing to do, on the face of it; if you've read this report and the EQUESTRIAN RED SIRLOIN dossier you might well be asking, "What the fuck, Bob? Why not send in a bomb-disposal robot instead?" And I will happily agree that if we had a freaking bomb-disposal robot to hand we'd do exactly that. Alas, they're all vacationing in Afghanistan this month—either that, or they're in storage in a barracks in Hereford, which does us precisely no good whatsoever. And we're clearly dealing with a many-tentacled occult incursion from the dungeon dimensions here, and those things eat electronics for breakfast. Much better to send in a warded-up human being: faster, more flexible, and I've got a couple of field-expedient surprises up my sleeves to boot.

For one thing, I'm wearing a borrowed helmet with a very expensive monocular bolted to it—an AN/PVS-14 night vision camera. Everything's grainy and green and a bit washed-out, and I can only see through one eye, but: in the kingdom of the blind, and all that. For another thing, I'm wired up with a radio mike and carry a crush-proof olive drab box under my arm. We're pretty sure there are no survivors in the building, which makes my mission all the more important.

For another thing—hey, don't worry, I've nearly finished reading my laundry list—I may not be a hero, but I'm not the fourteen-year-old H. P. Lovecraft either. Dealing with eldritch horrors is part of my day job. It's not even as bad as the paperwork, for the most part. True, the "moments of mortal terror" shtick really sucks, but on the other hand there's the rush I get from knowing that I'm saving the world.

And finally?

I'm more than a little bit *angry*.

So I walk into the booby-trapped woodshed full of explosives. Two guys with guns are waiting behind the door as it scrapes shut behind me. All I have to do is yell and they'll do a quick open-and-close, then cover my retreat. I plant the horrifyingly expensive mil-spec shockproof LED lantern on the floor. Right now, it's a brilliant flare of light in my night vision field, quite bright even to my unaugmented eye. Showing me precisely where to jump if, if, if it's necessary.

I take another step forward, stop, and call out: "Hey, Shub-face! I'm here to talk!"

The silence eats my words, but I can feel a presence waiting.

The air in the woodshed tastes damp and smells of mold. I take a deep breath, then sneeze as my sinuses swell closed. *Oh great*, I think: *I'm mildly allergic to elder gods.* (Only it's not a god. It's just an adult unicorn in the sessile, spawning phase of the life cycle. A very naughty unicorn indeed.)

"We've got you surrounded," I add, in a more conversational tone. "Broke your glamor, rounded up all your Renfields. Took down most of your sterile female workers."

(Because I have worked out this much: the thing I'm dealing with isn't just a sexually dimorphic *r*-strategy hyperparasite; it's a eusocial hive organism that can co-opt other species the way some types of ant domesticate aphids. And I've got another theory about the intelligence that Lovecraft called Shub-Niggurath— although I'm not sure he wasn't pulling it out of his arse, as far as the name-calling is concerned—and where it comes from.)

I take another step forward and nearly trip over something hard that's the size of a football. I catch myself and look down. It's a human skull. Fragments of flesh and the twisted remains of a radio headset cling to it. *Shit.* Well, now I know for sure where Alan's troopers ended up. I glance up.

The beams above my head support a layer of crude planks. It looks uneven and rough in my night scope. Odd trailing wisps of rotten straw dangle from it, as if a plant is growing on the floor above, pushing its roots between the cracks. Something moves. I stare, then look down as I hear a tiny *clonk*. A conical snail-shell as long as my little fingernail has fallen to the rough floor near the—*ick*, I glance rapidly away from the decapitated remains of the soldier. Then I force myself to look back. Wartlike, the snails rasp across the pitted and grooved body armor and fatigues, migrating towards the bloody darkness within.

"*Shub-Shub-Shub*," rumbles the huge and gloopy presence resting on the floorboards above my head. I jump halfway out of my skin, then step back smartly. There's a high-pitched squeal of rage and pain as my foot lands on something that skitters out across the floor: a tiny, gracile horse-shaped thing as long as my outstretched hand.

"Talk to me in human, Shub," I call, pointing my face at the darkness above. "I'm here to negotiate." *Here to hear your last confession*, I hope. Actually, I've overrun my safety point by a couple of paces—I should be standing on, or within three meters of, the door. But I need to find out if any of the troopers—or the little girl, Ada—are still alive. And I urgently need to find out just how intelligent this particular spawning unicorn Queen has become, to be laying gnarly plans to plant hundreds of fertile daughters on the population of a girls' boarding school, rather than allowing nature to take its course and seed a half-handful of survivors at random around East Grinstead.

"*Shub-Shub-Shub*," says the thing. Then, in a heartbreakingly high voice with just a trace of a toddler's lisp: "Daddy, why is it dark in here?"

My stomach lurches. The voice is coming from the attic.

"Daddy? Turn on the lights, Daddy, *please*?"

Lights?

I take a step back, closer to my safety zone, then swing my head round slowly. With the night vision monocular it's like having a searchlight, able to pick out details only in a very small area. Close beside the door, there—I see a mains switch and a trail of wire tacked to the wall.

"Daddy? I'm afraid…"

I skid across the unspeakable slime on the floor and push the switch, screwing shut the eye behind the night vision glass as I do so. The blackness vanishes, replaced by a twilight nightmare out of Bosch, illuminated by a ten-watt bulb screwed to the underside of a beam.

Yes, there are logs in the woodshed. They're piled neatly against the far wall, beyond the rickety stepladder leading up to a hole in the ceiling. There are also the partially skeletonized bodies of two—no, three—soldiers—

"Daddy! Heeelp!"

A little girl's voice screams from the staircase opening, and I realize I'm much too late to help her. Even so, I almost take a step forward. I manage to stop in time. I know exactly why those three troopers died: they died trying to be heroes, trying to rescue the little girl. I close my eyes briefly, take a deep breath of the mold-laden sickly-sweet air. Take a step backwards, to stand in front of the exit from the charnel house.

(There are two skulls on the floor—one of the bodies still has a helmet. They're on either side of the ladder. Part of me wonders how the thing in the attic decapitated them. Most of me wants to close my eyes, stick my fingers in my ears, and scream *I can't hear you*.)

"Talk to me, Shub," I call. "You want to talk, don't you? It's the only way you or any of your brood are going to get out of here alive."

The roof beams creak, as if something vast is adjusting its weight distribution. *"Shub. Shub. Glurp.* Daddy, it wants me to talk to you. Daddy? Will you come up here?"

I swallow bile and tense my leg muscles to flee. "No," I say.

"Shub! Shub! Shub!" The thing with Ada in the attic, the thing working her vocal cords, booms at me, a menacing rumble. Obviously, it's not happy about its latest self-propelled snack refusing to follow the lure upstairs. I use the rumbling as my cue to unhook the sample jars and look around. Her spawn crawls over the woodpile, near the dead and half-eaten troopers. Tiny horses and cone snails, swarming and chewing. I swallow again. Look sideways: near the door, a handful of snail shells crushed by boots. Survivors inch across the floor around them. I crouch down and use my forceps to take living samples, one per glass-walled tube. Snail, horse, snail, horse. They go back into the crush-resistant fiberglass box and I lock it and sling it over my shoulder.

That's what I'm really here for, you know. It was pretty clear that this was a zero-survivor situation once Alan confirmed that brick three was missing. But anything I can learn from the Queen...

"We have met before," the Queen says through Ada's childish larynx.

"Have we?" I ask.

"You remember me. I was your Hetty. I said we would meet again. Isn't that right?"

My skin crawls. I begin to frame a reply, then stop. I was going to say something human, but: *do not disclose operational intelligence to happy fun serial group mind horror.* I try again: "You wake up each time: reincarnation, isn't it? You find yourself fat and sleepy and spawning in a warm, food-rich place. And you remember who you were—who you are. Is that right?"

"I knew you would understand! Come close and you can join me."

Bingo. "And you keep trying to do better each time, don't you? What was the idea, this time?"

"Will you join me if I tell you? I will make you immortal and we will thrive and feed and dance joyous through the aeons—"

"Yes," I lie.

"It has been so long since I have mated with another mind... Yes, you must *join me! My idiot offspring eat their mother's flesh and then their siblings, before they mate and grow sleek and strong and seek out a nest and settle down, and I awaken behind their eyes. One or two in each brood prosper that way. But I have worked out a way for more to survive to maturity. Join me, help me, and we will be fruitful and amplify and become myriad."*

"I don't think so." I can't hold it back any more.

"Why won't you—"

"Your last worker is on its way home to visit, carrying your last Renfield. But it's not going to be allowed to get here, Shubby. We're not going to let you distribute your spawn via the girls at St. Ninian's. The school's on lock-down, and they know what to search for. Acid baths, Shubby. Anything that looks like My Little Pony is going to take a one-way trip through an acid bath and a furnace *on sight*. Snails, too."

A snarling animal scream cuts through the air behind me, from beyond the closed doors. It's cut short by a harsh chatter of automatic gunfire.

The thing above me roars in existential pain and heaves its bulk up, then brings it smashing down on the ceiling. Paint dust and splinters fall and the light bulb shakes, the shadows flickering across the room. *"My children! My beautiful future flesh! My babies!* Traitor! *I would have loved and cherished your memories forever!"* The snails and tiny horses swarm on the skeletonizing remains of the dead soldiers. Another voice cuts through the cacophony: "Dadd-ee! Help me!"

I step back towards the door. I tap my throat mike and speak quietly: "Got samples. No—" I glance at the ladder—"survivors. Over."

"Roger," Alan says calmly. "Target neutralized in yard behind you. Come on out. We're falling back now. Over."

I throw myself backwards at the woodshed doors. The ceiling creaks and screeches and then begins to buckle, giving way and drooping from the edges of the loft stairwell opening. Something huge is pushing through from above, something like the rasp of a slug the size of a bus, iridescent and putrefying and bubbling with feculent slime. It vents a warbling roar, *"ShubShubShub."* The door gives way behind me as I topple, getting a vague impression of writhing tentacles, a huge nodding eyeless horse-head, something like a broken doll impaled on a wooden stick—

Someone catches me and then I'm sprawling across a back as they pick me up and run across a farmyard, dodging around the fallen bulk of another of the horses from hell. I can see stars and a high overcast of cirrus whirling overhead as my rescuer pounds across the packed earth. Wall to one side, reflecting the livid glare of a burning building. "Get down!" someone shouts in my ear as he drops me on the ground in the lee of a drystone wall.

"Got it—" I scramble for cover as the incendiary fireworks surge overhead and the woodshed lights off with a *whump* I can feel in my bladder.

And then I lie there until Sergeant Howe gives everyone the all clear and sends a medic to look me over for triage, clutching the sample box like grim death and telling myself that it was all over for Ada Doom Edgebaston long before I walked through the woodshed door.

Because reincarnation only works for alien group mind horrors, doesn't it?

Keep telling yourself that, Bob. Take your sample tubes back to R&D in London, leave the burning wreckage of the farm behind. Take your cold comfort where you can, and keep telling yourself that the nasty thing old HPL saw behind the woodshed was lying or mistaken, and that you'll never meet it again.

Who knows? You might even be right...

HOME OFFICE
CONFIDENTIAL
Procurement Specification: HO/MPMU/46701

Date of Issue: May 3rd, 2006

Requirement for:

Enhanced-Mobility Operational Capability Upgrade Mounts for Police Mounted Units

It is becoming increasingly clear that in the 21st century mounted police are seen as an anachronism by the public. Despite their clear advantages for crowd control and supervision of demonstrations and public sporting events, mounted operations are expensive to conduct, require extensive stabling and support infrastructure, and compete for resources with other specialist units (e.g. airborne, tactical firearms, scene of crime investigation).

This document contains the operational requirements for upgraded genetically engineered mounts that will enhance the capabilities and availability of our mounted officers...

Desirable characteristics:

Mounts should exhibit three or more of the following traits:

- Endurance in excess of 6 hours at 30 miles/hour over rough terrain (when ridden with standard issue saddle, rider, and kit)
- Endurance in excess of 30 minutes at 50 miles/hour on

metaled road surfaces (when ridden with standard issue saddle, rider, and kit)
- Ability to see in the dark
- Ability to recognize and obey a controlled vocabulary of at least 20 distinct commands
- Invisible
- Bulletproof
- Carnivorous
- Flight (when ridden with standard issue saddle, rider, and kit)

State of Requirement

CANCELLED September 5th 2006

by Order of Cabinet Office in accordance with recommendation of SOE (X Division) Operational Oversight Audit Committee

Reason for cancellation order:

Sussex mounted constabulary has no conceivable operational requirement for sentient weapons of mass destruction.

This requirement document has no identifiable origin within the Home Office.

It echoes historic attempts to induce adoption of Equoid-friendly facilities within the armed services via requirements raised within the MoD. All of these have been successfully resisted.

It is speculated that someone is trying to pull a fast one on us: does Shub-Niggurath have a posse in Whitehall? This matter warrants further enquiry, and has therefore been referred to External Assets for investigation and permanent closure.